EARTH, GANYMEDE AND JUPITER –
THE BATTLE OF THE
THREE PLANETS!

There was a click. Fraser sat for a minute feeling oddly alone. Then he shook himself, rose, and walked toward the hall door.

It was flung open in his face. Pat Mahoney exploded through. His features were stretched into a Gorgon mask.

'Mark! Get out of here! They're arresting everybody who can operate anything!'

'What?' Fraser gaped at him.

'Those bastards from the ship – their goddam liberty party pulled guns and – they're taking over! For the old government!'

Also by Poul Anderson in Sphere Books:

THE BROKEN SWORD
THE AVATAR
THE PEOPLE OF THE WIND
THE MERMAN'S CHILDREN

Three Worlds to Conquer

POUL ANDERSON

SPHERE BOOKS LIMITED
30/32 Gray's Inn Road, London WC1X 8JL

First published in Great Britain by
Sidgwick & Jackson Ltd 1982
Copyright © 1964 by Pyramid Publications, Inc.
Published by Sphere Books Ltd 1982

TRADE
MARK

This book is sold subject to the condition that
it shall not, by way of trade or otherwise, be lent,
re-sold, hired out or otherwise circulated without
the publisher's prior consent in any form of
binding or cover other than that in which it is
published and without a similar condition
including this condition being imposed on the
subsequent purchaser

Set in Photon Times

Printed and bound in Great Britain by
Cox & Wyman Ltd, Reading

1

The guide beam reached out in answer to his signal and locked onto him. *Home again*, he thought. His hands moved across the pilot board, adjusting vectors more delicately than a pianist controls notes, until the moonship rode a true curve. The cabin throbbed with energies.

Raising his eyes to the viewscreen, he saw Ganymede as half a globe ahead of him. It was a cold sight, mountains like teeth, craters like fortress walls, their shadows long and lengthening across blue-grey plains. Though already nighted, just east of the John Glenn range, Berkeley Ice Field lay high enough to throw Jupiter light back at him, a sheening amber reach that lost itself around the curve of the world. Southwestward thence, slashing through the heights and a thousand miles over Mare Navium, the scar that was Dante Chasm ran toward the Red Mountains. Not far north of it, almost on the sunset line, Aurora's visual beacon was now visible, a green star that flickered on and off, on and off. But past the horizon, blackness was aswarm with other and older stars, unblinking diamond sharpnesses.

Not for the first time, he thought, *I'd like to know what's out yonder*. But he wouldn't live that long. And it didn't matter. There was sufficient mystery in the Solar System for a lot of human lifetimes yet – yes, and trouble and danger and hope, all scrambled together in life's careless fashion. Hope reborn on Earth just as hell was letting out for noon on Jupiter –

The radio buzzed. 'Aurora Space Traffic Control to Moonship 17, that's one-seven. Acknowledge,' said a familiar voice.

1

Startled, Fraser jerked in his seat, and laughed a bit at himself for doing so. 'Shucks, Bill, you needn't get stuffy with me,' he said. 'This is Mark in *Good Ole Charlie*. Remember?'

'Well – ' Enderby sounded sheepish. 'Ah, never mind. I was putting on company manners. But if any of 'em happen to be listening, let 'em think we're slobs. They'll probably be right.'

'Company? How's that?'

'You haven't heard? We told every outpost.'

'I wasn't at Io Base. Went directly to the mine, and flitted directly back here when my job was finished. So what's happened?'

'A battleship, that's what.'

'Huh?'

'USS *Vega*. Made groundfall fifteen hours ago.'

Briefly, Fraser's heart stumbled, and he had a sense of the hair rising on his skin. He shoved the tension down again, as far as he could, and managed to ask, 'What news?' in a level tone.

'Nothing much, from what I can gather. We've only seen a few of the personnel. According to what Ad-HQ announced to us, she was on patrol near Venus when the revolution broke, and was put to searching for an orbital base the Sam Halls were believed to have somewhere in that sector. Didn't find it. I don't imagine she looked too hard, if her commander had any sneaking sympathy for them. He seems to have had, maybe to have been in cahoots with them all along, because the *Vega* wasn't called straight home when the fighting ended. Instead, the new government ordered her here, to see if we needed anything and make sure of our allegiance.'

Still trying for calm – those had been harsh months while an intermittent radio beam sent tatters of information about the civil war ripping across American soil, a war that could

2

at any minute have gone nuclear; and the beam was cut off when Earth slipped behind the solar wind curtain, eight days after a still uncertain victory! – Fraser made himself picture the battleship's track. She must have taken a cometary to get here so fast: plunging as near the sun as coolers and radiation screens allowed, letting it swing her around, and then applying maximum blast. You gained considerable efficiency when you added gravitational potential energy to your jets. The saving in reaction mass would let you accelerate longer than usual, turn your eventual orbit into a still flatter and swifter hyperbola.

As always, he found engineer thoughts soothing. Forces and matrices were so much easier to deal with than people. 'Our allegiance is okay and then some,' he said. 'But I'd better write Santa Claus a long list of wants. My department's run low on Mark Four Everything, what with the last supply ship not coming.' *Well worth it, though,* his mind added. *A temporary breakdown in logistics, and any amount of belt tightening is small price for being free again.*

Why . . . I could go back home now . . . as my own man!

His eyes returned to the bleakness in the viewscreen, and for a moment it was blotted out by the memory of blue water and white foamcaps, a wind that tasted of salt, under Earth's lordly sky. But then his glance wandered, fell on Jupiter, and suddenly he was unsure. He had lived a dozen years beneath that storm-blazoned shield, and if Ganymede's rock and ice were hard to strike roots in, they gripped those roots all the more tightly.

'Well,' he said in haste, 'what's your call about, Bill?'

'Oh that,' Enderby said. 'With the battlewagon taking up so much room, we have to put moonships in a bunch at the north end. There are already several parked. You'll have to descend on a very, very finicking line, and manually. Can do?'

'Look, I inspect and service this pilot board myself. I can

put my boat down on the price of a Congressman.'

'R-r-roger.' Enderby issued instructions. Fraser listened with care, but had time to feel a little ashamed. The legislature and the courts ought to rate respect, now that the Army of Liberation had booted out the dictatorship. Wasn't that so?

Or was it? After this long a time at the far end of a four-hundred-million-mile communications line, a trickle of censored radio, censored letters, censored publications, how much truth could he know? Noble slogans were cheap, and the finest causes could go awry. Even the dictatorship had started as a movement to restore to a beaten United States her sovereignty and her pride. Then somehow one emergency after another cropped up, and those who grumbled began to have problems with the cops. . . .

His thoughts were swallowed up in the business of planet-fall. Meant to land at unpredictable points, the intersatellite carriers depended on their pilots as often as on auto-pilots. Not every person could acquire the necessary skills. Something had to be born into him.

When the last jet was cut off and the cabin had shivered to silence, Fraser unharnessed. He was a tall man, rather on the gaunt side. Forty years had put lines in his long jut-nosed face, around the grey eyes and wide mouth; the darkness of his hair had begun to frost over.

Putting the system on standby, he went aft to the space-suit locker. This far from the regular port facilities, a tube couldn't snake out for his passage into Aurora. He got the garb on fast over his coverall and cycled through the airlock, as impatient to see Eve and the kids as he was to see the newcomers. And call Theor, of course – find out how matters stood on Jupiter. It had infuriated him, having to run over to Io for a week in the hour of his friend's distress. But the automated mining establishments, here and on several other moons, were still a-building, and the colony's

4

chief cryogenicist was forever getting calls to come and trouble-shoot.

He unfolded the accommodation ladder and went down it as if into a pit. The other craft stood close around, stubby big-bellied shapes that covered the ground with the inky shadows of airlessness. He almost collided with the space-suited figure waiting by *Charlie*'s landing jacks, before he saw.

'Oh, hello,' he said. 'Can't make out anything through your faceplate, but hello anyway.'

A hand grasped his helmet and pulled it into contact. 'That is you, Mark, isn't it?' came Lorraine Vlasek's voice.

'What the devil! Why talk by conduction? Your radio out of whack?'

'Privacy.' The muffled sound had a frantic overtone. And his chief electronics technie wasn't given to dramatics. His throat tightened anew.

'Thank God you're back,' she said unsteadily. 'You're the only one I dare talk to.'

'Whatever's wrong?'

'I don't know. Maybe nothing. But that battleship. Why did she come here?'

'Uh, well, Bill Enderby said –'

'Yes, yes, yes.' Her words fell over each other in their haste. 'Does that really make sense to you? Maybe it does. You've been so long away from Earth. But I left only two years ago. Already then it was like a boiling kettle, subversive propaganda, security officers murdered, riots, raids, everywhere over the world. Is that supposed to stop just because there's a new government in Washington? They could have sent us a cargo ship. We're only five thousand men, women, and children, unarmed, not even equipped to leave the Jovian System. What possible danger could we be? And meanwhile every bit of American power is needed at home, if things aren't to explode.'

Fraser drew a long breath. His relief at finding her worries were empty ones turned him limp.

'See here, Lory,' he said, 'you're letting your prejudices — sorry, your opinions — run away with you. I can sympathise. I never blamed you for being so unhappy when we heard about the revolt, and I sincerely hope people will soon stop cold-shouldering you on that account. It's not your fault that the schools drummed into your generation that the U.S.A. had to mount guard on the entire human race, or there'd be another thermonuclear war. But damnation, foreigners *aren't* evil. They only resented our bossdom, as who wouldn't? Didn't our country resent the Soviet bossdom, so much as to finally destroy it? If the Sam Halls really can establish the kind of cooperative peace authority they promise, why, that solves the whole problem — and Americans won't have to enslave themselves any longer, either, just to sit on the lid. Stop shying at ghosts.'

'Oh, Mark! You're a good engineer, but you simply don't know — never mind. I'm scared. That story the ship's commander handed us is too thin. Seen from Jupiter, the solar wind interference doesn't cover so wide an arc that Earth is out of radio touch with us for more than a couple of weeks ... remember? Surely the government would wait that long and query us directly, before sending a ship that might not have been needed at all.

'And ... there's a guard posted around her, every minute. And you'd expect the crew to get liberty, to come in and fraternise, but they haven't! Except for a few officers, they've stayed inboard.'

'Hm.' Jarred, Fraser thought of his family, and of what a bombardment could do to Aurora. He wet his lips. 'But they must know we're on their side. Why the devil are more than half of us here in the first place? To do scientific research, sure, and the auxiliary work — but there're plenty of similar opportunities elsewhere, not quite so far out at the end of

6

beyond. No, we were damn well fed up with secret police and official uplift and labour drafts and censors and bureaucrats. We wanted to put as much space between us and Earth as possible. And the old government knew it, and was glad to cooperate in getting rid of us so easily and usefully. Everybody knew it.'

'Exactly. So why send a warship now?'

Fraser paused. In the silence of vacuum, his pulse and breath sounded feverish. 'I don't know,' he said at last, harshly, 'and I don't know what to do about it, either. Any suggestions?'

'Yes. Make some quiet preparations for getting out of town.'

He caught at her arm, gauntlet against brassard, and blurted: 'What do you expect will happen?'

'I've no idea. Maybe nothing. Maybe I'm being hysterical. But . . . oh, I did so want to talk with you.'

She hasn't anybody else, he realised. Which was odd. No other girl had remained single for two years, in a settlement still overloaded with bachelors. He patted her awkwardly on the back. 'Well, here I am, kid, and what I have to say is, don't be such a worrywart. Let's go on in, huh?'

Perhaps she nodded. He heard the hum in his earplugs as she switched on her suit radio.

The *Vega* was huge. She could never have touched on Earth, and now that Lorraine had raised the question of motive, he did think it odd that she had not taken an orbit around Ganymede. A five-hundred-foot spheroid, grey paint scored and blistered by radiation and micrometeorites, rifle turrets and missile tubes and boat locks humping dinosaurian athwart the sky, she seemed almost to fill the concrete apron of the regular spacefield. That was an illusion, he knew, and so was the impression of overwhelming mass. She was a shell, thinner than any civilian vessel, relying on speed and firepower for protection against

7

weapons that made any armour futile. But nonetheless he felt as if a mountain had descended, and the land looked suddenly strange to him.

Unconsciously seeking familiarity, he gazed around. Westward the Sinus Americae stretched beyond sight, losing itself over the near horizon before it opened on Mare Navium. The sun hung low above Navajo Crater out there, winged with zodiacal light, the disc shrunken to a fifth of its homeside angular diameter but still too bright to look at. Eastward the lava plain lay equally bare and dark, save where the monorail to the ice mines slashed a metal streak; but the highest peaks of the John Glenns thrust into view. Northward the Gunnison made a jagged wall, ramparts touched with radiance. Over them, over everything arced the night of space. He couldn't see many constellations. Though Ganymede gets only some four per cent of the illumination that Earth does, the human eye is so adaptable that the country does not seem especially dim, and the pupil narrows so much by day that none but the brightest stars shine through. But Jupiter was plain, of course, vast and cloudy brilliant in half phase, a little south of the zenith.

'Cha-arge!' he said, and struck off with the long flat strides of low-gee. He took a secret pride in being able to move so lightly at his age. Not that he enjoyed regular calisthenics. He swallowed a euphoriac pill before each dismal session. But you had scant choice in the matter if you wanted to stay healthy in a mere eighteen per cent of Earth's gravity field.

Passing near the ship, he noticed the ring of armed and armoured sentries. *Oh, hell,* he thought, *they only have an ultracautious skipper.* Trying to shake off his unease, he glanced past them, down to the west end of the field. The *Olympia* was still there, her big clumsy-looking shape a comfort and a promise.

Unless . . . His eyes strayed to the planet in the sky. 'Any word from Jupiter while I was gone?' he asked.

'Yes,' Lorraine said. 'Pat Mahoney told me that your friend, that prince or whatever he is, called about fifty hours ago and wanted urgently to talk to you. Somebody on the lingo team told Pat, and said none of them could make out the reason why.'

She spoke absent-mindedly, her concern more with the guns that shadowed her. Fraser swore. 'That must mean heap big trouble. I'd better contact him right away.' His fists drew together. 'Though what can I do?'

Beyond the field, they zigzagged through a portal in the safety wall and confronted Aurora. Apart from some outlying domes for special purposes, the town was four long slabsided sections, eight stories high, forming a quadrangle in whose courtyard the main radio mast lifted its beacon-eyed skeleton. The building material was native stone faced with white sealplast. There was no reason to burrow underground here, as on Luna. Solar weather was too remote to be a hazard, and if you took your Antion on schedule you didn't need to worry about biological damage from cosmic rays. Meteorites posed a theoretical danger, though no big ones had struck this neighbourhood in the thirty years since men started colonising. If any did, interior compartmentation would minimise air loss. And it was worth the slight risk to save on power. Heat was lost to vacuum at a considerably lower rate than it would have been conducted away by Ganymedean rock, at two hundred or more degrees below the Fahrenheit zero.

Someday we'll warm that rock with nuclear energy, and crush it into soil, and blanket it with atmosphere, and turn this whole world green. An ironic part of Fraser reflected that it wouldn't be done for particularly idealistic reasons. There was so much to learn in the Jovian System that a permanent research base was a scientific necessity; which meant there had to be an extensive life-support plant; which

9

in turn meant a sizeable population of technies; who, like many of the scientists, wouldn't settle here without their families; and so the colony mushroomed. You had to hydrocultivate most of your own food, dig and refine your own metal, for supply ships couldn't come very often. And every further gain in economic independence meant a substantial saving in haulage costs. The logical ultimate goal was to make Ganymede into New Earth.

Still, motives weren't important. Nothing is as dead as the last generation's practical politics. The thing itself was what mattered and would endure, blue sky, blinking lakes, forests that rustled and rippled in the wind, under Jupiter. Sometimes Fraser woke from a dream of his childhood's ocean, and his pillow was wet.

He jerked out of his reverie. 'Stop mooning, you.'

'What?' Lorraine said.

He realised he had spoken aloud, and flushed. 'Nothing. Though, come to think of it, a bad pun. . . . Damnation! If Theor's people are overrun, it'll set our work back twenty years.'

She regarded him a while, until they stopped before an airlock. 'Don't kid me,' she said then, quietly. 'I've watched you pace the floor as the bad news came in. Those Jovians mean more to you than a scientific project.'

Surprised, a trifle embarrassed, he returned her look. She was a big blonde girl, too strong-featured to be pretty but with one of those figures that can knock out both a man's eyes if the owner sticks to her diet. He had found her competent and likeable. He could even stomach her politics, since she had by instinct the nearly forgotten art of not equating dissent with treason. She also had a sense of humour, and didn't mind working peculiar hours, and – until the revolution came to split loyalties apart – had been more heartily in the town's social activities than his own bookish self. But that was about the extent of his knowledge concerning her, before today.

'I guess so,' he mumbled, and turned the handwheel to undog the outer door. 'Now don't stew about that ship. Everything's going to be okay. Uh, would you stow my gear for me, please, and buzz my wife that I'll be hung up at JoCom for a while? I've got to call Theor. God only knows what's busted loose there.'

2

He settled himself before a microphone tuned to the band reserved for Jovian communications. 'Theor, this is Mark,' he said, not in English or Nyarran, for neither race could form all the sounds of the other, but in that language of croaks, grunts, clicks, and whistles which had been hammered out during two decades. Like every human attempt at a Jovian word, his voicing of the name was a crude approximation. 'Can you hear me?'

His sentences departed as a series of electronic waves. Some distance from Aurora, a radio transmitter picked them up and sent them out on a beam automatically aimed at whichever of the three relay satellites in equilateral orbit around Jupiter was handiest. On arrival, recoded into pulses, the words became instructions to a highly specialised accelerator. Bombarded nuclei fluoresced with gamma rays, which struck certain crystals, isotopically pure, bathed in liquid helium, each atom oriented by the grip of electric and magnetic fields. Their own nuclei took up the energy, surged for wild picoseconds, and regained peace at the cost of emitting a neutrino burst.

Invisible, impalpable, chargeless and virtually massless, that cone expanded toward Jupiter at just less than the speed of light. By the time it got there, it was wider than the equator. A million miles beyond, it had scattered to inherent undetectability. But it survived long enough.

The tightest, hardest-driven maser beam could barely have gotten past the storms of charge and synchrotron radiation where atomic debris surged in the king planet's enormous magnetic field; then punched through an atmosphere churned by thunderstorms often larger than Earth, an air packed down by two and a half terrestrial gravities until the pressure at the bottom exceeded the pressure in the Mindanao Deep. It could never have pierced a many-layered globe whose ice and metal and solid hydrogen amounted to two million billion billion tons. But so ghostly was that neutrino wind, so vast were the empty spaces it found not only between the atoms but within each single atom, that it swept through almost as if the obstacles did not exist.

Almost: not quite. Somewhere on the Jovian surface, a minute percentage of the particles entered another crystal. The latter was not identified with the transmitter crystals in the satellite; but its nuclei underwent a swift reversal of those processes which had given birth to the beam. They were extremely special isotopes, continually excited by a radionuclide to so high a pitch of instability that a mere few neutrinos would make them jump back to a lower energy state, giving up quanta as they did. Nature provided such neutrinos, of course, but not so abundantly – because resonance was also required – that the background noise was intolerably high. The quanta came out in bursts corresponding to the pulse code of the beam. A solid-state device, drawing its own power from the built-in radioactivity, amplified the signal, mapped it onto an alternating potential, and made a little piezoelectric sheet vibrate. The receiver, a thick four-inch disc, spoke with the voice of Mark Fraser.

Some of the finest minds the human race ever brought forth had spent a generation making it possible.

'Theor! Are you there, boy?'

He should be, damn it. He carries the gadget around with him constantly these days.

Unless he's dead. Fraser took a worn briar pipe from a

13

pocket and began to fill it from his pouch. Never mind if he used up his tobacco ration before the next shipment came. His hands shook.

In a darkness that human eyes would have found absolute, another hand moved. A button was pressed. A voice said gladly, 'Is that you?'

Crystals vibrated, electrons leaped, and some of the energy from the disintegrating isotope became a radio signal of extremely great wavelength. In this unearthly environment, matter was forced into strange allotropes by pressure, chill, and its own composition, and the wave was conducted over the ground. It was feeble indeed, but an artificial thing, with hardly any natural competition. Its effective range was therefore on the order of a thousand miles. Well before it had gone that far, it activated another neutrino generator. Again, this was a device which was not, could not possibly be like its counterpart in orbit. Besides the fundamental differences required by Jovian conditions, it was a broadcaster, not a beamcaster; for though the moons eternally turn the same hemisphere to their primary, Jupiter rotates in five minutes less than ten hours. Thus the pulses which arrived at the relay satellite were far weaker than those which had left it. But the humans had detectors more sensitive and amplifiers more powerful than anything they had been able to land on the surface. The radio beam was modulated and flashed to Aurora.

'Is that you?'

Fraser's pipe dropped from his fingers. It fell so slowly that he scooped it up before it hit the floor. 'Yes,' he stammered idiotically. 'I – I – I hope I didn't disturb you.'

In the seven seconds that must pass between Q and A, he mastered his nerves. *What are you getting so worked up about, you gnatwit? Okay, so Theor's a nice chap in his unhuman fashion; and if his enemies swamp him it'll put a crimp in our projects – but still, how can anything on that*

14

planet make any serious difference to me or mine? Jupiter's more alien than Hell itself.

'No,' Theor said. 'I should have dimmed my consciousness long ago – night is now where I am – but with so much future to plague me, I cannot. Well that you called no later, mind-brother. The race and Reevedom stand in high need of your help.'

'Couldn't you get help from, uh, my colleagues?'

Fraser felt more than a little touched. You couldn't work together for almost a decade, as Theor and he had done, with an objective which amounted simply to understanding each other, and not build up a sense of comradeship. He had admitted to himself, quite some time past, that this creature of cold and gloom and poison chemistry was closer to him than most humans.

'I strove to convey the wish, and surely they desired to comprehend, but always our discourse flowed about and turned in on itself.'

Fraser grunted with astonishment. 'Do they have so poor a savvy at this end? I hadn't realised.'

Wait a bit, though. He'd never kept close track of how the Jupiter-study teams were doing. Ten years back, while helping improve the transceiver system, he'd gotten so interested that he began to spend his spare time talking the crude pidgin, which was the best they had then, at any Jovian willing to reply. Before long, he was holding regular bull sessions with Theor, who'd gotten just as bugs on the subject. The chief of the language research group in Aurora was happy to let Fraser do so. Every man-hour was valuable, especially when the engineer and the prince made more progress in developing a mutual code than anyone else had done. (That, no doubt, was because of sheer persistence rather than innate talent. Over the years, they subconsciously picked up clues to the nuances of each other's personalities.) Their recorded conversations swelled the data files.

15

'Nor I. My demi-father Elkor, as well as numerous philosophers, have had much exchange with your staff in the past. Yet neither they nor I could thrust comprehension across, in this matter of our present necessity.'

'Um-m, I think I see why. It hadn't occurred to me before, but every other man who knows common-language is a scientific specialist, asking questions about those few particular aspects of your world that interest him most. So their effective vocabularies are still pretty narrow. Language involves more than words. There has to be some rapport as well – a feeling for how the other guy thinks. And Jovian and human minds do differ. You and I, we just rambled in our conversations. As a result, we've developed a broader range of subjects that we can talk about with more fluency than anyone else on either world.'

Old Ike Silverstein would never have gotten so over-specialised. JoCom was the child of his dream, his begging and bullying megabucks by the thousands from a reluctant government, his nursing the teams through heartbreaking years of R & D in areas of physics that didn't exist before him, until the first instruments were successfully softlanded on Jupiter. They were crude small things, their maser telemetry so distorted by interference that little could be read. Silverstein flogged his crew into designing better ones. And when those sent back data to prove there was intelligent life on the planet, he worked himself to literal death in birthing the communication project.

'Your thoughts are well built, Mark, and I believe they support a truth. But our inwardnesses may not fare abroad this night. Time is thin before the Ulunt-Khazul arrive.'

'What's happened? The last I heard, you'd sent an army against the invaders.'

Joe Dahlbeck, who took over from Silverstein, would have understood Theor too, and probably outlined a winning strategy for him as well. He was the necessary universalist. Engineers could only design scanners, receivers, transmitters that would continue to function after the murderous Jovian atmosphere had corroded their vehicles away; and money could only provide so many machines that eventually one must land near a Jovian settlement. After that, it was up to genius — the kind of genius that can start with arithmetic sums in beeps and end with a verbal language. True, the Nyarrans included some sharp intellects, who'd worked hard also, once they got the idea. But Dahlbeck had been the semanticist who finally saw enough of the basic structure of the Nyarran glossa that he could know how to go about developing an Esperanto for the two races. . . . Seven years ago, his gannycat veered out of control and went down a cliff on Mount Schirra. Now a routineer was in charge of the linguistics team.

Though it would probably have deteriorated anyway, after the *Olympia* project started. So much glamour attracted all the most original-minded young men. Fraser even caught himself in occasional daydreams about riding that ship.

'Yes,' Theor said. 'We thought this was only another barbarian incursion, and dispatched the border guard to rout them. Instead, they cut our people to fragments on the shore. Survivors relate that their host is immense, and not even of our race. Two different breeds of thinking animal have met.'

'What?' Fraser whistled. Then: 'Well, I suppose that figures. On a world as big as yours, with travel as hard, you might well get more than one intelligent species. Though I suspect you're of the same genus.'

And how could men dare land the *Olympia* at Nyarr, if that city, the sole part of Jupiter about which they had anything like exact knowledge, was ruined and overrun? Oh, they could go ahead and take a chance; or they could pick another area arbitrarily; but the enterprise was hazardous at best. To multiply risks was sheer foolishness. So the ship stood completed and idle.

'No matter that,' Theor said. 'Apparently they crossed the western ocean by way of the Floating Islands. Our own traders keep an outpost there, or did. If the Ulunt-Khazul captured that, they could have learned our language and much about our country from the people there. No doubt they have also secretly scouted our shores. Now after the battle we sent envoys to ask for discussions, more in the hope of probing out information about them than because we fear to fight. However, I confess to fearing the outcome if we do fight. They agreed, and their representatives will arrive in the city two days hence.'

'That's only about twenty hours. No wonder you were getting frantic. But what can I do to help?'

Silence hummed while the neutrinos leaped back and forth. Fraser's gaze flickered around the cluttered room. It felt suddenly stifling.

'You know with what awe your machine that spoke was received by us,' Theor said. 'In fact, to some degree it changed the nature of the Reeveship, back toward the ancient function of conductor in magical rites; for of course my kin-tree was the most active in dealing with the thing and groping toward a language. You will recall that we took the image-maker you sent us a third of a year ago – ' that would be four Earth-years, Fraser reminded himself – 'to a special shelter near the House of Council. This shelter has become known as Iden Yoth, the House of the Oracle, and many believe that prophecies are uttered there. Yet we are not a fanciful people in Nyarr city or across the plains of Medalon. Barbarians should be more prone than us to visionary interpretations.'

'Ah . . . yes! I see. You want me to – '

The intercom blared: 'Your attention, please! This is an announcement from Administrative Headquarters, Bob Richards speaking. Admiral Swayne, commanding the bat-
18

tleship out there, just called to ask if he could send a large liberty party inside. Naturally, that's fine by us. So if you want to entertain any of these boys, now's the time to make ready. Over.'

A shaky grin lifted one corner of Fraser's mouth. *So much for Lory's fears*.

'What was that?' asked Theor anxiously.

'Nothing important,' Fraser said. 'Let's go back to your affairs. I agree, the sight of me might well scare the hypothetical pants off any Jovian who wasn't prepared for the shock. I suppose you want me to give the barbarians a suitably gruesome warning of what'll happen if they don't leave your territory.'

There was a clatter from the adjacent laboratory. No doubt the fellows were shutting up shop for the rest of this watch period, so they could go out and greet the spacemen. Fraser paid no heed.

'You engulf my thought,' said Theor. 'I have an intuition that this may swing the balance. The Ulunt-Khazul must know that there are lands to the north, less rich than Medalon but more easily taken. If they are brought to fear supernatural vengeance, as well as seeing how great a host we can muster against them, they should rationally decide against invading us.'

'Um-m, I'm not sure how their minds work. Even you don't always make sense to me, and here we've got another culture – another species, in fact. Still, I'll do my best. Only how? Your enemies don't understand the mutual language, and I can't speak Nyarran.'

No man could. Perhaps nobody would ever be able to. The problem went much deeper than differences in vocal organs. Dahlbeck had established that Nyarran was not one but three interrelated systems, each with a different set of underlying premises: as if a human should mingle English, Chinese, and Hopi. And all those hidden assumptions about the nature of the universe were abstracted from a racial

19

experience totally foreign to man's.

'I know. But I can recite the speech for you, here and now, and you can record it, and send it back with your image upon the day.'

'Excellent! I'll have to know what it means, so I can make appropriate gestures as it raves on. Do you have a script prepared?' Fraser lit his pipe and blew cheerful clouds. Things seemed to be looking up everywhere, on Jupiter as well as Earth and Ganymede.

'I have a tentative structure. But I would like to discuss the whole with you. I am sure you can make many suggestions of value. Besides, your cast of thought and phrase will lend a strange flavour that should add to the impressiveness.'

'Great! I can show films too, if you think that's a good idea. Let's get to work.'

They finished more than an hour later. Fraser was surprised to notice the time. *Hope Eve hasn't gotten too irritated with me.* 'Very well,' he said. 'I'll stand by, here, at your conference time. When you want me to start transmitting, call. That should sound like an invocation or something to your guests.' He paused, awkward again. 'I do hope this works, Theor.'

'Your mind-nearness brightens existence. Farewell, friend.'

There was a click. Fraser sat for a minute feeling oddly alone. Then he shook himself, rose, and walked toward the hall door.

It was flung open in his face. Pat Mahoney exploded through. His features were stretched into a Gorgon mask.

'Mark! Get out of here! They're arresting everybody who can operate anything!'

'What?' Fraser gaped at him.

'Those bastards from the ship – their goddam liberty party pulled guns and – they're taking over! For the old government!'

20

3

Without instruments, no man could have seen morning on Jupiter. At the bottom of that monstrous atmospheric ocean – mostly hydrogen, much helium, a few percentage points of methane, ammonia vapour, and other gases – the only visible illumination on land was from the frequent great lightning flashes. Then cloud banks might stand forth in miles-high red and tawny precipices, until blackness clamped down again. But Theor's two eyes, golden in hue and thrice the diameter of a man's, saw by infrared as well as the longest red wavelengths. To him, a brightness climbed swiftly out of the night mists that still rolled across Medalon, tinting them in a thousand rich shades, spreading across the vast, roiling arch of the sky. He felt wind in his face, sharp and cold; the chemosensor antennae flanking his mouth quivered as they drank organic odours blown off the plains.

He wished he could merge himself again with the year, sink back in the work and the rites which were his to lead, as heir apparent to the Reeveship. His mind continued to worry those problems he had been dealing with until this last possible minute. The druga species were undergoing their regular metamorphosis from vegetable to animal, and the ranchers who kept such herds had a thousand attendances to dance on them. This meant that other tasks must be neglected, which meant that wind, rain, hail, lightning, quake, flood, geyser, firespout, stonecrush could wreak havoc unless certain precautions were taken. Those it was Theor's job to direct. . . . That was the basic function of the

21

Reeve and his kin-tree. Only incidentally and occasionally were they priests, magicians, judges, military leaders. Always and forever they were the master engineers. Without their skills, in an environment so riven by elemental forces, Nyarr would soon return to barbarism.

As could happen anyhow, Theor reflected grimly. *We can stand off the raiders from Rollarik with little effort, for we are more than they, and more cunning and better armed; and then they have to cross the Wilderwall in the first instance. But these newcomers − ! Who brought so huge a force the whole way across the ocean!*

That shook him at least as much as their fighting prowess. Nyarran ships coasted south to trade with the Foresters; they harvested the sea near Orgover; a few expeditions had gone as far west as the Bright Islands. But how was it possible to cross the thousands of miles of storm-swept liquid ammonia that reached beyond? Theor knew the distance was that much to the next piece of land big enough to hatch a host like the Ulunt-Khazul. The Earthlings on Ganymede had learned it from their probes and passed the information on.

His eyes went heavenward. He had never seen the moons, or even the sun. Strange if Nyarr should be saved by help from a place invisible and unreachable. Though to be sure, Mark had told him that those moons raised air tides and thus controlled the Four Lesser Cycles. . . .

'Ulloala!' The voice came from below, travelling fast and far in the dense medium. 'Theor, I see you, descend for discourse!'

'Ush?' Startled, he drew on the reins of his forgar. The mantis-like beast slowed its flying − or swimming − and slanted downward. The rider stood on its broad back, feet braced in four stirrups.

He was still some ways from the city, able to see both the wide, bright curve of the River Brantor and the red-tinged smoke from Ath. Those villagers must be hard at work now, smelting water over their volcanic outlets – the only kind of fire known on Jupiter – to forge weapons. He peered ahead. A slender form in a blanket dyed pirell and onsy stood waving a plume-tipped staff. Theor recognised his demi-father Norlak. What was he doing out here?

The Reeveling landed and jumped off. His forgar settled to cropping the spongy-leafed bushes roundabout. The soil in which they grew was ice powder, intermingled with organic matter and minerals that were chiefly sodium and ammonium compounds. Theor felt it crunch under his feet as he advanced.

'May the Powers be serene within you,' he greeted formally, then went over to the patois of practical affairs. 'We've small time. The enemy delegation must be in town.'

'They are,' Norlak said. 'In fact, they arrived late yesterday. But I thought I'd best talk matters over with you beforehand, so I came out to intercept you.'

'Why aren't you at the meeting? It may already have commenced.'

'They said that by their law only males could attend councils. If we insisted on having any others present, they'd break off negotiations at once. Elkor and I decided to swallow the insult.'

Theor nictitated in surprise. The three sexes were substantially equal in Nyarr, though the placid temperament of the females, and their normal preoccupation with the young, kept them from desiring much voice in affairs. The wild folk of Rollarik had a somewhat different arrangement, and the Foresters still another; but this was extreme.

'Indeed,' Norlak went on, 'the Ulunt-Khazul chief remarked that their females are kept as property, and most of their demimales are killed at birth – only a few spared for reproduction. Their host is entirely male. After they've conquered us, he said, they'll bring their other sexes from the

23

Floating Islands, where they're waiting.'

Theor grimaced. 'Now I know they're another species, not just a different race of ours.' He tugged thoughtfully at his antennae. 'This might work to our advantage, though. You demimales may be more excitable than males, but you're also quicker-witted.'

'True,' Norlak said with a touch of smugness. 'Was it not my idea that we get your sky-dwelling friend to frighten them? I wish I could be present, to observe the enemy reactions and guide their emotions. Males don't have any real sensitivity to such things. Most of your wits are in your hands.'

In past arguments, Theor had maintained that this was a libellous exaggeration. After all, he was the one who had established communication with Mark. Norlak always retorted that that was more through male doggedness than male intellect. But only a light-minded demimale would indulge in banter at a time like this. Theor shook his head, which meant what a shrug does to a human, and asked, 'What did you want to tell me?'

'My recommendations for your behaviour, since I must be absent myself. Also, what I've been able to learn about the Ulunt-Khazul. You shouldn't meet them for the first time without some background information. Our mistake was in assuming them to be a mere barbarian horde. It cost us the initial engagement. They're something much more formidable.'

Theor composed himself to listen.

A man seeing those two Jovians would doubtless have thought, *Centaur*. But that was too crude. Theor's hairless red body, stub-tailed and tiger-striped, did stand upon four stout legs; but each foot had three prehensile toes. His long arms, four-fingered hands, and blocky torso might be considered anthropoid, if one overlooked innumerable details. But his round head lacked external ears and bore a rooster-like comb, fifty inches above the ground. The mouth sat

24

close below the great eyes, and was only for eating and drinking. Speech came by vibrating muscle tissue in a pouch under the jaws.

He had no nose or lungs in any terrestrial sense. Half a dozen slits on either side of his thorax, with lips to close them at need, let hydrogen diffuse inward, where his metabolism employed it to obtain energy by reducing organic compounds whose ultimate source was vegetation. The methane and ammonia given off by this process came out through abdominal vents. At Jovian air pressure, the system was efficient enough to support a large, active animal.

Except for a tool belt and the communicator disc hung from his neck, he was nude. Being homeothermic, and living on a planet whose slight axial tilt makes for less temperature variation than on Earth, Jovians rarely had any practical need to dress.

However, Norlak's sex went in for gaudy clothes. The demimale was short and slim. He lacked a comb, his antennae were longer and more acute – an interminable list of differences might have been compiled. Male and demimale must both impregnate a female, within a few hours of each other, for conception to result. With genetic diversity thus increased, evolution had proceeded about as fast as it does on Earth, despite the lower mutation rate in this cold and weakly irradiated environment. A mother gave live birth and fed her infant by regurgitation. In Nyarr, a three-way marriage was considered permanent and exclusive. Other societies had various other ideas.

Including the Ulunt-Khazul arrangement. Theor was shocked by that concept. And such creatures meant to swarm across Medalon? He was less combative by nature than a man, but the thought made him clench a hand on his hammer.

'I've been piecing together what scouts and survivors of the battle can tell, besides my own observations of the

25

embassy,' Norlak said. 'The Ulunt-Khazul homeland seems to be low and swampy, scattering off into the ocean as island clusters. You'll see for yourself how the people are built to be swimmers, and evidently they became master shipwrights. We know they can cast ice. They found their way clear across the ocean, which means they're better navigators than us. In fact, they invented the compass by themselves, while we had to get the idea from Ganymede.' There was some lodestone, like other metal, on the Jovian surface, of meteoritic origin and more rare than diamond on Earth.

Norlak voiced the equivalent of a sigh. 'We must face the fact,' he said. 'They aren't barbarians. Their civilisation is radically different from ours, but almost as complex and sophisticated.'

'Hurgh,' said Theor. 'Then they may be hard to scare with the Oracle.'

'At least, you'll be wiser to threaten supernormal rather than supernatural vengeance.'

'Which will make certain passages in the warning difficult to rationalise.... Yes, I wish you could be there, demifather.'

'Well, being only males, they may not be impossibly hard to bluff. But I think you should stay closer to the facts, treat the sky-folk as carnate beings rather than Powers ... though of course you'll omit the fact that they can't come here themselves.'

'Mark said – ' Theor broke off. That was no use at present. 'What made the enemy leave home?'

'A weather belt shifted to their country. Storms caused famines.'

'Yes, Mark explained that to me once. Where two bands of the upper air meet, rotating at different speeds, they breed a region of unrest which –'

'Spare me. I'm hardly the Reeve type. To continue, the Ulunt-Khazul have scouted us out in some detail. People

26

caught glimpses of their spies – now I know why so many rumours were flying a cycle or two ago, about the Hidden Folk faring abroad – but in a land as big and thinly settled as ours, the glimpses were few. They must also have interrogated elsewhere. Altogether, they have a good idea of what we and our country are like. Their bluntly announced intention is to dispossess us. Now at the meeting today, you should – '

Norlak went into a long speech. Theor listened with an impatience that grew. The ideas were good, no doubt, but time was shrinking. In the end, he said only: 'Yes, yes, I'll do what I can. The need is for action, though, more than planning. So I'll be on my way. Peace abide with you.'

He swung himself onto the forgar and lifted skyward before Norlak had a chance to respond.

Several minutes later he descended at Nyarr. From above, the city looked more like a scattered stand of copses than anything else. Houses were pits, with thin interior walls that wouldn't crush the dwellers in an earthquake. Their roofs were living plants, so densely interwoven as to be weatherproof while yielding enough that the winds could not tear them off. A similarly thick hedge of thornbush grew tall around the town. Ships lay empty at the riverside docks, and the paths between houses had an ominous lack of their usual bustle. Most folk were indoors, waiting.

He landed in the square between the House of Council and the House of the Oracle, and hastened toward the former. Three troopers guarded the entrance. They wore armour of scaly kannik hide and carried spears whose heads were alloyed ice – a dense, hard mineral at this pressure and temperature of minus 100 degrees. 'Halt!' barked one. Then: 'Ah, you, Reeveling. Go on in. We wondered what had become of you.'

'How goes the meeting?' Theor asked in formal-phase words.

'Ill. They have only scorned Elkor's threats, and jeered at

27

his proposal that they settle in Rollarik.'

'Here's my son now,' came Elkor's voice from within.

'Hungn!' said a deeper, harsher, thickly accented tone. 'So even common spearwielders may listen to us talk.'

Theor went down the ramp and through an antechamber to the main room. It was lit in the common way, by phosphorescent blossoms growing among the leaves overhead. But it was bigger than most, a circle bounded by tiers on which stood the male elders of the country: ranchers, artisans, merchants, as well as philosophers. The sense of tension was an almost physical thing.

Elkor the Reeve stood alone on the floor with the half-dozen Ulunt-Khazul. He was still erect and powerful in middle age; but they dwarfed him.

Theor's gaze went to them and rebounded. He had heard them described, but the actual sight was jarring.

A human would have seen little difference: about as much as a Jovian would have seen between a man and a gorilla. The Ulunt-Khazul stood a foot taller than the Nyarrans. Small tusks grew down over their chins. Their feet were broad and webbed, they had long thick tails, their skins were shining grey. But every angle and every proportion was alien, some subtly, some grossly. And the smell from them was acrid – *animal* – Theor thought in disgust, then wondered how he smelled to them.

They wore hooded mantles, and two of their group sported bracelets that must have been looted off Nyarran dead. Worse, they had brought their weapons along, into a peace-holy place. Theor's hearts contracted with anger.

'We had nigh despaired of you, my son.' Elkor said. 'I was about to show them the Oracle myself.' His own radio disc protruded from a pouch in his tool belt. 'But now – Chalkhiz, warmaster of Ulunt-Khazul, know that this is Theor, the most intimate of us with those powers that dwell beyond the sky.'

Norlak had mentioned that the enemy chief had come in

person. It argued both fearlessness in him and a horde so well organised that his death would not be a serious blow. Theor met the chill eyes and said:

'Knowing so much else about us, you must have at least some inkling of our alliance with them. I don't pretend that we enjoy this because of any special merits of our own. But I do say that we are useful to them, and therefore favoured by them, and that they won't stand idle and let us be destroyed.'

Chalkhiz widened his mouth in a carnivore's grin. 'Then why have they let us invade you?'

'We did not ask for their help erenow.'

'We've heard many old females' tales in our wanderings – about spirits, and hobgoblins, and Hidden Folk, and these prophet voices of yours. The Ulunt-Khazul believe what they see, and little else.'

'Then come and see,' Theor retorted.

Following Norlak's advice, he turned on his heels and walked unceremoniously from the room. A buzz of surprise went along the tiers, and even the foreigners must have been taken aback. But they followed him after a brief hesitation, up the ramp and across the square and down into the House of the Oracle.

Two of them stopped short and barked something in their own language. A neutrino transmitter is an impressive sight even if one belongs to a society that builds such things. And then the long dim chamber was crammed with relics, fragments of disintegrated carrier vehicles, telemetric instruments they had brought down, pictures of space and Earth and humanity formed in perdurable crystals. The grey warriors gripped their weapons and moved close together.

Chalkhiz rapped a command. They put on an air of defiance. He himself paced restlessly about, picked up an object, set it down, crumbled a bit of metal between his fingers and held it to his antennae, stared for many minutes at the control panels. His face was unreadable.

'Well?' said Theor.

'I see some curiosities that might overawe a savage,' Chalkhiz grunted.

'You will see more. One of the sky-dwellers has agreed to appear and warn you.' Theor reeled off the account of them which he had prepared, as revised by Norlak. Chalkhiz's visage remained impassive.

Having finished, Theor went to the visual transceiver. It was not, of course, a conventional Earthside 3V, but a solid-state device, as nearly everything sent down to Jupiter must be, and it had rather poor definition. Today that might enhance the effect.. . . . He activated it with fingers that were not quite steady.

'I assure you most solemnly that to challenge the skydwellers is to invite destruction,' Theor said. 'I shall ask this one to show you living pictures of what he can wreak. Attend in silence while I invoke him.'

Chalkhiz poised rigid. But did his fellows shudder, ever so slightly? Hope jumped in Theor.

He pressed the button on his disc. 'Mark,' he chanted in the mutual language, 'this is the moment. They are here and horrible. Are you ready?'

The screen stood blank.

'Mark, are you ready for me?'

The ground rumbled and shivered. A soughing went through the roof leaves.

'Mark, they are waiting. This is Theor! Is anyone there? Hurry, I beg of you!'

' – Mark – anyone – '

' – Mark – '

Presently Chalkhiz began to utter those bass purrs that were Jovian laughter. When he left with his warriors, Theor was still shouting into emptiness: 'Where are you out there? Why do you not answer? *What has happened?*'

4

This:

'You're crazy,' said Fraser's reflexes.

'No.' Mahoney leaned on a workbench and struggled for air. A red lock of hair was plastered to his forehead with sweat. 'I saw. . . . I was in South Hall B, headed for the main entry lock . . . to watch 'em come in . . . oh, they did. A squad up the ramp, pistols in their hands, Clem and Tom and Manuel and two or three others with arms raised, walking between 'em. They saw me as they came onto the landing. Manuel . . . yelled at me, "Get out," he yelled, "they're taking over for the old gover'ment" – and one of 'em clipped him on the side of the head, and . . . the leader . . . aimed at me and said, "Halt! In the name of . . . the law." I was near the corner, so I says, "Whose law?" while backing away a little . . . and he says, "The gover'ment o' the United States" . . . and I backs up some more and says, "We got no trouble with it," and he says, "I mean the lawful gover'ment, not the rebels – " And then he sees what I'm doing and yells, "Halt or I shoot!" But I'm so close to the corner then, I swung myself around. Heard the bullet smash into the wall as I started running. Sounded like a fist. I ducked into the nearest crosstube and – we gotta jet, Mark!'

Fraser sagged back down into a chair.

It wasn't real, he thought dimly through the hammering. Couldn't be. Such things happened only on the 3V. No such crude melodrama, in his quiet life.

Although, there'd been the time in Calcutta, during his military service. His unit had been flown there to help put down the anti-American riots. Yes, that had been crude

31

enough to make him vomit, when flamethrowers were turned on the mob.

Or Professor Hawthorne, back when he, Mark Fraser, was in college. Too old and famous, apparently, for the secret police to cart off – at least, the game wasn't worth the candle, since he confined himself to teaching his own version of history – but he did assign passages from Jefferson and Hamilton and Lincoln in preference to Garward, and what was more annoying, he made his students tell him what those writings implied in practice. Oh, yes, the young toughs who burned his books and worked him over were entirely unofficial, and the police promised to investigate, but Professor Hawthorne died of internal ruptures anyway. That was fairly melodramatic, wasn't it?

Usually correction was gentler, of course. They took young Olson out of the chem lab one day, charged with distributing subversive pamphlets. He came back some weeks later, and his views were quite different, but he wasn't much good as a chemist anymore.

And even that was exceptional. Mostly you heard and saw nothing, except praises of our farsighted leader President Garward and his firm but benevolent administration. It got sticky after a while.

Fraser shook himself. Suddenly he wasn't tired. His body seemed to thrum. What had Lory said? 'Make some quiet preparations for getting out of town.' Too late now. But – 'Yes,' he said. His thought leaped ahead of the words. 'They must need this place for some purpose. If the rebellion had been suppressed, they wouldn't. So ... Clem, Tom, Manuel, all technicians, potential troublemakers, could send a radio beam to Earth a few days from now, or sabotage operations. Uh-huh. A squad should be here any minute. Let's go.'

He surged from the chair, two jumps to the exit. Strainingly cautious, he opened the door for a peek. The

32

corridor lay empty and still. 'Come on,' he said. 'If we hurry, we can grab a cat and escape.'

He started off to the right. 'Not that way,' Mahoney objected.

'I've got a family,' Fraser said.

'Well . . . yeah, you do. Okay.'

They got into a freight elevator. It hummed downward with the slowness of a Chinese torture. Fraser became aware of his heart slamming blood through ears and throat, the reek of his own sweat and its wetness under his arms. It was incongruous how steadily his finger had pressed the button for ground level.

The hall there was full of people. They wandered about in little huddling groups, not fast, bewilderment in their eyes and in the stiff, pale faces. A mutter went among them. 'Hey, Mark,' a man called, 'what's going on? You know? Somebody said – '

Fraser ignored him. He wanted to run – you could move like a scorched comet in low-gee – but the crowd was too thick, and he had to elbow his way through the molasses of nightmare. Time approached forever before he reached his apartment.

The door was locked. He beat on the panels. 'Jesus,' Mahoney said, 'if they aren't here – '

'Then you go on alone,' Fraser said. The saliva was thick in his mouth. 'I can't leave them here, can I?'

The door opened. Fifteen-year-old Colin put down the chair he had raised over his head. 'Dad!' he blurted.

'Mother and Ann here?' Fraser went through with Mahoney and shut the door behind him. Colin made a jerky nod. 'Suit up, everybody. Quick!'

Eve came from the inner rooms. She was a small woman, dark as her husband, the eyes enormous in her delicate features. Ann, born ten Earth-years ago on Ganymede, followed close behind, cheeks streaked with tears. 'I saw some Navy men go by carrying guns,' Eve husked. 'They –

33

I thought it was best we wait here for you. I couldn't raise you on the phone. It's dead.' Her hands closed on his. They might have been carved in ice. 'What can we do?'

'Leave town,' he answered.

'We – we – we might get killed!' Ann wailed.

Fraser cuffed her. He was instantly sorry, but his voice said for him: 'Shut up and get your suit on!'

Numbed, they turned to the lockers. Fraser checked the spares and pointed at one. 'That should fit you,' he told Mahoney. 'Not like your personal one, of course, but I'm afraid you'll have to make do.'

Eve hesitated before the outsider. 'No time for modesty,' Fraser said. 'Take off that dress and put on your coverall.' Mahoney turned his back as Eve yanked the garment over her head. Fraser had an instant – not of desire, there was no chance for that, but a memory of desire and of shared years. She'd given up more than he, to come here; politics meant little to her; but there had been no complaints. 'Good girl,' he said with overwhelming tenderness.

He donned his own suit. The fabric was stiff around him, the outside gear – aircycle tank, water bottle, belt of food-bars, sanitary box, powerpack, repair kit – an unexpected weight. He left the helmet open and the gauntlets off. Being already in his Long John, and more practised than the rest, he finished the clumsy process first and had a few seconds to look around. He might never see this place again.

It was cramped and austere, like every dwelling in Aurora, but Eve and the kids and he had made it theirs. Booktapes crowded the shelves, a half-finished spaceship model of Colin's overflowed a table, a chess set stood by Fraser's tobacco jar. He'd always liked chess and poker too much for his own good, he thought in the back of his brain; they could become a way of life if you didn't watch them. His gaze went to a colourstat over the couch, a view of the Gulf Stream. The water was nearly violet, and gulls made a white storm in the sky. But on some nights the sea would

34

phosphoresce, he remembered, you dipped your hand into the waves that lapped against your boat and lifted it with fire streaming off. . . .

That was his boyhood, on a sea station, a floating village where they herded whales and harvested algae and had horizons unknown to the poor crowded billions ashore. And because the working staff included people from several countries, and the station had no secret police and was too close-knit a community for anyone to fear being informed on, it had been an ill preparation for his later life. When at last he came to Ganymede, he felt like a man emerging from a submarine whose air renewal was out of order, going topside into the wind.

'All set, I guess,' Mahoney said.

'Where are we headed, Dad?' Colin's voice cracked ludicrously. But Fraser liked his expression. The frontier beyond Earth bred some damned fine kids, if they survived.

'To one of the outlier stations,' Fraser said. 'That battleship is seizing us on behalf of the Garwardists. But her crew can't occupy more than Aurora, I'm sure. Once beyond the Glenns, we'll see if anything can be done about them.'

Ann squeezed her eyes shut, drew an uneven breath, and said, 'L-lead on, Macduff.'

'Lay on,' Fraser corrected automatically. 'Now stick close behind me. Pat, you bring up the rear. Watch for bluecoats, but if you see any, don't run. They might shoot if you did.'

He stepped back into the hall and started for the nearest garage, forcing himself to walk at an even tempo. The passageway had emptied, doors lined it blank and strange, boots hit the hard floor with a noise that rebounded from grotesquely pastel walls. *What's gone on while I was inside?* he wondered.

He turned a corner. A spaceman stood halfway down the other corridor. He was a thick man, the azure uniform and white belt snug around him. There was a firegun in his arms. He swung it up. 'Halt!' His voice smashed at their eardrums. 'Where do you think you're going?'

Fraser stumbled backward. 'Home,' Eve said.

'Huh?'

'We just got in from the Mare. One of your people told us to go straight home and stay there, so that's what we're doing.'

'Okay. Move!'

Eve tugged at Fraser's sleeve. He followed her blindly, the opposite way from the guard's post. When they had made the next turn, Mahoney whistled. 'Good work, lass! How'd you figure out what to tell him?'

'If nobody was in the halls any more, they must have been ordered inside,' Eve said. She bit her lip to hold it firm.

'Daddy,' Ann attempted, 'maybe we better – '

'Nuts to that,' Colin said.

Mahoney opened the door on a downward ramp. Aurora had a basement level, for storage of whatever didn't mind being cold. Dank air flowed around them. As Fraser closed the door again, he saw his breath smoke white under the fluoropanels.

'Suppose they've put a watch on the garage already,' Mahoney muttered. 'Then what do we do?'

Fraser ducked into a toolroom. He came out with a hammer and a couple of pipe wrenches. 'You, me, and Colin,' he said.

'Against a gun?' Eve protested.

'If necessary.' He didn't quite know why. He certainly wasn't any hero. He'd never even considered joining the underground. To be sure, it was much smaller and weaker in his youth. Still, that was perhaps the reason why he had to fight now.

'Ann,' he said, 'you're obviously harmless. Can you go ahead of us? If there's a guard, talk to him. Draw his attention. Can't be more than one. I'm certain.' He took her by the shoulders and looked down into the eyes that were so much Eve's. 'It's a tough thing to ask of you, Nellyboo,' he said harshly, through unshed tears. 'But you're a brave girl.'

The short thin form crept close to hug him. Despite the spacesuits, he could feel how she shivered. 'O-Okay, Daddy,' she got out.

Eve gripped Fraser's hand as their daughter went before them. They walked in great silence, nearing the cross-corridor to the garage.

Ann stopped at the turn. The shout from beyond seemed to push her back physically. 'You, there! What's the matter with you?'

'I can't find my daddy,' Ann wailed, and ran toward the voice, out of Fraser's sight. 'Please help me to find my daddy!'

Fraser gestured at Mahoney and Colin. They edged to the corner. Ann's hysterics mingled with the guard's orders, which began to take on a desperate note.

'Now,' Fraser whispered, 'Jump out and pitch!'

He made a bound of his own, to the opposite wall, whirled on his heel and let the hammer fly. The wrenches came an instant later. They often played baseball on the field outside Aurora.

The bluecoat went down, hit in face and stomach. He struggled to his knees, cursing in an astonished voice. His gun came up. But then the others were upon him. What followed was short and ugly.

When he lay still — breathing yet, but Mahoney had smashed his head several times against the floor and the breathing was ragged — Ann fell into Fraser's arms. He comforted her as well as he could. But half his mind was on the spaceman: a young fellow, as nearly as could be made out through the blood and the broken features. Decent by nature, no doubt; he hadn't fired on the little girl — Colin snatched the laser gun and Mahoney the sidearm. 'We'll want these,' the boy said theatrically. His eyes glittered. Fraser tried not to remember the boys, scarcely older, who had destroyed Professor Hawthorne.

'Quick,' Eve begged. 'We may have been heard.'

'Right.' Fraser gave her Ann to carry. They went through the door into the broad, echoing space of the garage.

The gannycats stood in rows. Each was a big squarish machine, with a clear dome on top, alternately retractable wheels and treads below. The power accumulators were always kept charged, the supply lockers filled. Fraser opened the nearest and herded his party in.

He took the controls himself. The cat glided up the ramp and into the airlock. While he waited for chamber exhaustion, Fraser began to shake. *We can't really have made it!*

'Here,' Eve offered him a pill from the vehicle's medicine chest. He swallowed with difficulty. But the psycho-drugs went to work fast. By the time the outer lock door opened, he felt like a storybook warrior. His senses were acutely aware of his entire universe, Mahoney and Colin crouched on their seats, Ann cuddled in Eve's arms and Eve crooned to her, the cold air that puffed through his nostrils, the purr and forward thrust of the machine.

The stars, as he rolled forth. Night had fallen, and space glittered with suns, uncountable in their multitudes, the Milky Way a chill cataract, Europa horned above the black spires of the Glenn peaks. The city shone bone-white, the battleship loomed over the safety wall like a monstrous fallen moon. And overhead Jupiter had entered third quarter.

The planet glowed. Fifteen times the diameter of Luna seen from Earth and incomparably brighter, it dominated the sky, deep amber banded with copper and cobalt and malachite, the titanic roil of the South Tropical Disturbance invading a night side that had a dim glow of its own. And it

38

filled the plain with light. Dark lava on Ganymede shimmered; a glacier edge peering over the eastern range seemed to dance beneath the stars. *Why do I miss the ocean so much, when I have this?*

Fraser swung the cat toward the Glenns. Beyond Shepard Pass were a number of minor settlements, one family or a few, digging metals from the Uplands or ice from Berkeley Field. 'It's okay,' he said. 'Everything's under control now. We'll have you safe in just a few hours.'

'Nah,' Mahoney said. 'Nobody'll be safe till those sods yonder have been taken care of. But we're better off out of town, sure.'

No formal road had been built. Fluorescent lines drawn across the rock marked a negotiable route. Two miles would put Aurora under the horizon of a tall man. Even before then, Apache Crater would hide a cat from view. It bulked sheer ahead, ruined battlements shining under Jupiter but the foot in total shadow.

The receiver, automatically tuned to the general band, cleared its throat: 'You! In that cat bound east! Halt in the name of the law!'

Fraser twisted his neck around and peered backward. *Credit the pill for any coolness I can show at this juncture.* Slowly he identified the shape, a vehicle similar to his, a mile behind.

He switched on his own transmitter. 'What's the trouble?'

'You know damn well what. That sentry you attacked was found. We've got a squad of armed men in this car. Halt.'

Pat Mahoney's skin glistened wet in the Jupiter light that poured through the dome. But he made a rude noise. 'Your cat's no faster than ours, and we're used to driving on this terrain,' he said. 'Run along home, sonny.'

'Can you travel faster than a bullet or an energy beam, traitor?'

5

The ships of Nyarr came down the Brantor and out into Timlan Bay, where they swung north. Standing on the after deck, Theor looked across long grey waves to the shore. There the land army moved, a red mass of ranchfolk with spearheads nodding and glittering above, banners snapping in the low wind. Forgar riders cruised overhead, zigzag beneath tawny clouds. The baggage train followed, a mile of loaded kanniks – vaguely like six-legged, squamous tapirs – and some that pulled carriers. These were not wagons; because of poor roads, wheels were little used on the queasy Jovian surface. They were boxes slung beneath houlk logs, whose interior expansion on heating turned them buoyant in the air. The sound of footfalls came to Theor as one remote drumroll, over the wave-noise and the splash and creak of the ship's paddles. Beyond the army, the land sloped bush-covered until the plains of Medalon lost themselves in mist and distance.

'Well,' he said needlessly, 'we're on our way.'

He was desperate to forget his wife and demi-husband he had bade goodbye at sunrise. She had not spoken her thoughts much, but she caressed him very often, as if to seal his memory fast in every sense. And she was carrying their first child.

'We should be able to whip them,' he said. 'Norlak, you must have finished reviewing the different estimates of their strength. How greatly do you think we outnumber them?'

'Sixteen per sixty-four, at least,' his demi-father answered. 'Still, they are fighters by trade and our folk are not.'

Elkor's eyes ran over the ten octad or so ships of his fleet. He waved at a forgar rider, who swooped low. 'Go tell the captain of *The Beak* to close formation.'

The black lozenge flitted off. 'Why so fussy?' Norlak asked. 'We won't reach Orgover for days.'

'When we do,' the Reeve said, 'we will be glad to have had some practice in maintaining a line.'

Down in the well that ran fore and aft, the watch was being changed. Crewfolk got wearily off the treadmill and climbed gangways to the deck, where they stood slumped. Briefly the ship wallowed before the seas. Then the replacements began walking. The belt turned beneath them. The paddlewheels flanking the broad hull bit deep, the steersman trimmed his rudder, and the vessel ploughed on.

Given the long-barrelled Jovian build, as well as the relatively small free-board available in liquid ammonia, it was a more efficient system for a large galley than oars would have been: especially since the wheels served as outriggers, no mean advantage on a planet where waves travel some sixty percent faster than they do on Earth. The Nyarrans were acquainted with sail, but did not use it much, winds being ordinarily slow in so dense and feebly insolated an atmosphere.

'We've been peaceful too long.' Elkor said. 'A few hundred border patrollers sufficed to hold back the barbarians. It would be better for us now if the Wilderwall did not exist, so that everyone in Medalon knew how to fight.'

'That's a bleak logic.' Norlak grimaced.

Theor felt less taken aback. The Reeveship meant growing up in one kind of war that never stopped.

Though there was a difference, he confessed to himself. The violence of a flood bursting a levee, a field suddenly turned into a volcanic pit, a landslip laying a village in wreck, was not the same thing as another mind actively seeking one's death. He tried to strengthen his resolution

41

with memories of hunting expeditions – there had been dangerous game to face with no more than a spear or axe for weapon – but nothing came back to him except the chase, the exuberant thrust of muscles under his skin, cloven air roaring around his head, bushes that gave way with a crack and a whipstroke, as he galloped over a plain that had no limits. He hoped he would not be afraid when battle broke.

His forebodings could not very well be put in human terms. A man carries half the sex of his race, Theor only a third. He was an individual, with his own personality, and he was self-aware, but both to a lesser degree than the typical Homo Sapiens. What troubled him was not so much fear of being hurt as a sense of wrongness. That which had happened and that which was going to happen should not, and shook him on a purely biological level.

The treadmill gang struck up a chant, it lifted into the air together with the sharp smell of their labour and the throb in the deck:

'Right, one! Left, one!
Right, one! Left, one
Never mind where you're going or why.
Feels like we're pushing her into the sky.
But don't you go hoping the ocean runs dry,
BE-cause
THAT ain't
Right! One! Left, one!
Swing 'er around and no matter the toil. –'

'Suppose we are beaten,' Norlak murmured.
'I do not care to suppose that,' Elkor said.

'Feels like the ocean has started to boil.
Coxswain, the wheels and yourself need some oil.

AIN'T that
JUST so
Right? One! Left, one! –'

Norlak fidgeted with his staff. 'There are other lands. We could go –'

'As a broken remnant? How many sixty-fours of years did it take our ancestors to subdue this one country? We could become nothing but another barbarian tribe – no, not even that, for we have lost too many arts of the barbarian.' Elkor's crested head lifted. 'Better dead!'

Theor moved away from them. No doubt his male demi-father was right, but he didn't care to be reminded of such choice. As he walked down the gangplank to the main deck, and on forward through the off-duty crewfolk, he took a stringed instrument from a pouch in his belt and plucked it. The tune ran back and forth under the verses from the well, a melody dedicated to birthtime, as close to a sentimental ballad as anything Nyarr had.

No one was on the foredeck but a lookout. Theor ignored him, drifted over to the figurehead and leaned against its intricate shape. The harplet quivered in his fingers.

'Theor!'

He dropped the instrument. It smashed on the deck.

'Theor, this is Mark. Are you there?'

He snatched at the locket. 'Yes, oh, yes.' His pulses thuttered while he waited for response.

'Are you all right?'

'Thus far.' His sense of balance returned, and he spoke more calmly than he would have expected. 'Yourself?'

Some seconds later: 'Likewise.' Fraser chuckled rather grimly.

'What has happened to you, mind-brother? You did not answer at Iden Yoth.'

'I'm sorry as hell about that. But at the time, I was too

43

busy staying alive. What happened when I didn't reply?'

'The Ulunt-Khazul scorned my pretensions and departed. Now we have no choice but to fare against them, hoping to shatter them at their beachhead before they move inland. I myself am aboard a ship.'

'Eh? You're attacking by sea as well as land?'

'Yes. Our feeling is that they will not dare let their fleet be taken from them, but will divide their forces, some to fight our vessels and some ashore. Since we have numerical superiority on the ground, this may offset their advantage of greater size and skill.'

'Is there any chance – look, I could stay where I am, with access to a radio. The main transmitter in Aurora automatically relays messages on the Jovian band, and I don't think the enemy will shut it off. Why should they? It won't occur to them, I hope. So, if you could get the invaders to talk some more in the near future, back at Nyarr –'

'I fear not. At least not until we have inflicted a defeat on them.' Anxiously: 'But what is your story?'

'Not a pleasant one. You remember my telling you that the government on Earth was overthrown?'

'Indeed. I have often tried to make sense of the concept. How could a leadership maintain itself in the first instance when not to the benefit of the people?'

'A lot of them thought this one was. But some of us felt freedom was more important than security.'

'I also do not quite grasp the intent of those words. However, continue, I ask of you.'

'Well, a ship landed at Aurora. We believed she was friendly, but then her crew swarmed in and captured the town, on behalf of the old overlords. I don't yet know what the situation is, whether the war has flared up again on Earth or what. But I decided I'd best get out with my family. We, and a friend of mine, got a vehicle and fled toward the mountains.'

44

'Ah, so,' Theor said when Fraser paused. Briefly he wondered if he might be making a trip like that himself. He dismissed the thought. 'But you have many times said that your race cannot lived on Ganymede without artificial aids.'

'Yes. We were headed for the small settlements on the far side of the range. Well, the enemy saw us escaping, and another vehicle set off after us, with several armed men in it. When we refused to stop, they began shooting at us. We closed our spacesuits and kept going, even after our cabin was riddled and airless. Hoo, what a ride! We dodged through every cleft and every patch of shadow and around every ridge and crater we could find. If we hadn't been used to travelling on Ganymede, as they weren't, we'd never have survived. But we did get up onto Shepard Pass, where we could broadcast a distress call. About that time, our cat was wrecked by a couple of lucky shots. We abandoned it and took off on foot. Found us a cave – we had a couple of guns – stood siege for several hours. Help didn't arrive any too soon.'

'Did you not say once that you settlers lack weapons?'

'Uh-huh. But a laser torch can double as a gun at close range, and a blasting stick can be thrown quite a distance here. The Hoshis saved us, one man and his sons. They took care of our opponents, and brought us to their house. We're there now. I'm using his radio, a beamcaster aimed at the nearest relay tower – but you don't care about that. I had to get in touch with you, Theor, as soon as ever possible and find out . . .' Fraser's voice stumbled and trailed off.

'Your silence has lasted for days. Was your flight that long?'

'N-no. I was probably in the cave just about when I was supposed to play oracle. But frankly, I keeled over after the rescue. And then, well, we had to call the other outliers first, warn them, plan for a counterblow.'

'Do you think that possible?'

'I don't know. It had better be possible, that's all.'

Theor looked ahead, into an illimitable northward darkness. The prow bit into a wave and spray sheeted cold across him. He braced himself against the pitching and said slowly: 'So our battles come at the same time, yours and mine, and each helpless to aid the other. What Powers have we crossed?'

> *'Right, one! Left, one!*
> *This is a hell of a wet place to be,*
> *Walking to nowhere, alone on the sea.*
> *Lightning just scribbled a letter to me.*
> *SO, dear,*
> *WHY not*
> *Write? One! Left, one!'*

6

The room was large, walls of undressed stone, furniture hewn from the same rock and decked with cushions. A round port, salvaged from a wrecked spaceship, opened on the north. The Uplands stretched rough and dark out there, pitted with shadow where small meteorites had gouged craters out of granite, until chopped off by the sheer cliff of Berkeley Ice Field. It rose a hundred feet, that cliff, shimmering greenish yellow under the radiance of waning Jupiter. Samuel Hoshi's ice mine was visible at the base as a skeletal crane and a shed that protected machinery against cosmic bombardment. The installations looked pitifully small against such a background, beneath so many frostlike stars.

He got up from his chair, a stocky man with muscular flat features and a grey crewcut, and went to the 3V. 'Time to hear what Admiral Swayne has to say,' he declared into silence.

'Huh!' snorted Tom, the oldest of his five sons. 'I wouldn't trust him even to keep to the announced time of his announcement.'

'Oh, that is the one thing you can trust,' Pat Mahoney said. 'I know his breed.'

One of Hoshi's youngest grandchildren began to cry. Her mother got very busy soothing her. The women and children sat on the benches at the farther wall, as if to hide from the screen. The men gathered close to it. Colin Fraser was with them, but kept near his father.

Mahoney laughed. 'Simply by being here, he's made conformists of us,' he said. 'On every moon where anybody is, every place is tuning in at the identical moment.' No one stirred. 'Okay,' he shrugged, 'so I never will make a good comedian. Of course, a comedienne, now . . .' But that fell flat too.

Mark Fraser turned his pipe over and over in his fingers. His mouth cried out for a smoke, but he couldn't keep on bumming from the Hoshis. Could he?

The older man snapped a switch. The screen lit up. Fraser's pipe fell into his lap. Lorraine Vlasek was looking out at him.

'. . . important declaration,' the husky contralto voice said. 'I was asked to go on first, representing the civilian population, which means each one of us in the Jovian System. You aren't going to like what you will hear. But on behalf of your families and neighbours, I beg you to listen calmly. In times like these, we can't do anything but follow our legitimate leaders.'

'Good God!' Mahoney exploded. 'I knew Lory was a sucker for the Garward line, but I never thought she'd collaborate!'

Fraser shook his head. He felt a little sick. 'Nor I.'

'She might have decided there was no choice,' Eve said gently. 'That ship could destroy Aurora with a barrage, couldn't it?'

'Quiet, please,' Hoshi said.

'. . . commander of the USS *Vega*, Admiral Lionel Swayne.'

Lorraine's face slipped out of the screen. The camera panned in on a man seated behind a desk. He wore dress uniform, his shoulders glittered with insignia and his breast with decorations, but a Spartan impression remained. Perhaps that came from the stiffness with which he carried his slender frame, the gaunt grizzled head, or the eyes, blue and as unwavering as the stars of space.

48

'My fellow Americans.' He spoke surprisingly softly. 'I have come to you in an hour of tragedy, the darkest hour of our country's life. Once again she is torn by the strife of brother against brother. Once again, nothing can save her but the courage and dedication of a Lincoln, the iron will of a Grant.'

'When's he gonna get around to home and mother?' Colin muttered. *Good lad!* Fraser thought, in spite of the words that struck out at him:

'But this is a time of yet greater danger. For this is the time of the unleashed atom. The United States was the ultimate victor in the period of nuclear wars, but you know what it cost and you know how near she came to annihilation. Had the Soviet empire not fragmented, while our own people stayed loyal to their cause, nothing would be left of her but a blackened waste through which barbaric aliens would still be pouring in search of land and loot. Having, however, by God's grace gained world hegemony, the government of the United States had no alternative but to impose peace upon a chaotic planet. No other sovereignty could be allowed to exist, for any might loose the nuclear demon upon us without warning. And so the United States fulfilled her destiny. She became the protector of the human race. You grew up in that stern but just peace. Your children were born under it. But you have seen the radio-active ruins. Do you want the wars back?

'Of course you don't. The will of the American people has expressed itself time and again, whole-heartedly for peace, security, and wise leadership. Was not the Twenty-Second Amendment repealed, was not President Garward repeatedly re-elected by majorities of more than ninety percent, did Congress not unanimously vote him the title of Protector, and vote him, too, the official thanks of the nation for his far-seeing statesmanship? You know the answer.

'But now you know also that a band of traitors existed in our midst. Nurtured in the bosom of America, this poisonous clique nonetheless turned upon her. Over the years, in space, and with the clandestine help of foreign governments, the Sam Halls built up their strength. And at last they hit. Their ships landed on the soil of the motherland, their shells tore her, their boots trampled her, their wheels ground her. Surly at being deprived of the decisive weapons, ungrateful for the peace that they too had enjoyed, the foreign countries refused aid to the lawful government of the United States. Seduced by propaganda, not a few of our own citizens turned Benedict Arnold after the landings and joined the pirate flag of Sam Hall. Far too large a majority of the rest were passive, trying only to keep out of harm's way, as if their precious lives mattered more than their country's. The rebels had certain new weapons which gave them a strong advantage in conventional operations. And our leadership was too merciful to employ nuclear force against them.'

That's not exactly the way I heard it, just before Earth went behind the sun, Fraser thought. *According to the new government, the nukes were withheld because the revolutionaries had some, too. Garward wouldn't have gained anything if he tore the country to pieces. Only, at the end, when defeat was plain to see, he did order the missiles flown – and one of his own officers shot him.*

A muscle knotted in Swayne's cheek. 'You have heard the result,' he said. 'The traitors triumphed. They sit in Washington at this moment. Their agents are hounding down the brave men of the Security Police, on whose work the entire world protectorate depended. Their legislature is tearing down a structure of law and regulation which is vital to internal discipline. Their generals are recalling our garrisons abroad. Their diplomats are negotiating treaties for a new peace-keeping system on what they call a basis of international equality. I call it by its right name: international *in*equality, dishonour, betrayal, the kiss of Judas. The wars taught us how far we can trust anyone beyond our own borders. Now the revolt has taught us that we dare not trust even our own people.

'This – must – be – stopped. For the sake of the entire human race, the Sam Halls must be overthrown, a legitimate successor to the great President Garward must be installed, and the American peace must be reimposed upon the world.'

He paused. His gaze continued to smoulder out of the screen. 'Does he really *believe* that?' Fraser asked aloud.

Hoshi nodded. 'Uh-huh. That's the most horrible part.'

Swayne rested his elbows on the desk. His metallic tone changed, became dry and almost conversational:

'You naturally wonder how my ship comes into this. I'm going to be perfectly frank with you. If I weren't, the truth would soon come out anyway. But that isn't my reason. I want your help, willingly and loyally given, and I can't expect that of you until you know precisely what the situation is.

'The *Vega* was on patrol when the insurrection began. We were ordered to search for an enemy orbital station. It would have helped a lot if we'd found the thing; but we didn't. We could not have done much at Earth anyway. You're aware that a battleship is too big and fragile to land on a planet with an atmosphere. Nor could we have fired nuclear missiles from orbit. In the first place, as I've explained to you, the legal government didn't want to destroy a lot of innocent Americans along with the guilty ones. And in the second place, space warcraft don't carry atomic weapons in peacetime. Our chemical shells and rockets are ample to deal with other spacecraft. We had no chance to rearm, for the enemy captured the Lunar arsenal on the first day and could interdict any attempt to ferry weapons up from Earth.

'Well, the surrender came. All Naval units were ordered back for demobilisation. I conferred with my staff. Our crew had been carefully chosen for loyalty. They would carry on the fight if they got leadership. And I am deeply proud to say that not one of my officers proposed yielding.

'But what could we do?'

Abruptly the ascetic face tightened, the voice rang:

'This is my decision. Ganymede has a good-sized industrial plant. You mine your own fissionables, produce your own fusionables, and generate your own atomic energy. We have occupied Aurora and declared martial law throughout the Jovian System in the name of the rightful government of the United States. As you know, Earth will soon be accessible again by radio. The bandits in Washington will hear an account from our colonist friends of how everything is peaceful here, and how you are in no urgent need of supplies. The Sam Halls will have quite enough to do, on Earth and the inner worlds, without dispatching a costly expedition to Jupiter when none is required. If by any chance a vessel should approach, she will be detected at long range by the *Vega*'s orbiting boats. A missile will destroy her. On Earth they will assume the loss was accidental.

'All in all, we loyalists should be able to keep the Jovian System isolated for about three months. That is our estimate of the time it will take to produce the nuclear weapons we need. Then we shall destroy your main transmitter – regretfully, but you will understand the necessity. Under top acceleration, we shall return to Earth.

'With her new armament, the *Vega* can, in a few surprise blows, knock out the bases from which hostile craft might be sent, and defend herself against what few units may be in space at the time. I shall then deliver an ultimatum, that the outlaw regime lay down its arms or face atomic bombardment.

'If we must, with sorrow in our hearts but with steadfast will to do our duty, we shall bombard. But I do not believe the need will arise. The people themselves will rise and force out the traitors. Loyal elements now silent will make themselves known, will take control and re-establish order. We shall have done what honour demands of us. And so shall you, who made those weapons for us. No community in the solar system will be so glorious as yours.

'But make no mistake. This is war. Treachery will not be tolerated. Already some have fled this city. Several men of the *Vega* – men in the uniform of their country – have been killed. The perpetrators will be arrested and shot. Every expression of unfaith will be suppressed with the utmost severity. You, the people of the Jovian System, are now soldiers in the army of the right. The obligations of the soldier have been laid upon you. I must remind any traitors that even without nuclear weapons, the *Vega* has the power to annihilate every settlement on every moon. Do not think for an instant that men who are prepared to strike a cleansing blow at their own home soil will hesitate to use such power here.

'God willing, there will be no occasion to do so. God willing, the people of this colony will work side by side with the gallant men of the *Vega*, for victory – an American victory!'

The camera lingered on Swayne a minute and shifted away to a projection. The Stars and Stripes fluttered in a wind that had blown half a billion miles away, and the anthem crashed forth.

No one stirred in Hoshi's house.

Lorraine Vlasek came into view. 'You have heard Admiral Swayne's proclamation,' she said. An unnatural steadiness armoured her tone and the strong fair face. 'Speaking for the interim colonial government I would like to discuss what this means –'

Hoshi jumped up and snapped the image to extinction.

53

'I'll leave the recorder going,' he said, 'but right now I can't take any more.'

'The man's insane,' Eve whispered from the shadows where she sat. 'One ship against the whole Earth – he can't!'

'Insane, perhaps,' Fraser heard himself reply. 'But they might carry it off at that. The situation will be chaotic for months to come, back home, until the new government has got firmly established. If its centres are smashed – or the people may well revolt, in sheer panic. Do you remember what nuclear warheads can do? A thousand megatons exploded at satellite height will set half a million square miles afire simultaneously.'

'Even if he tries and fails, there might not be much left of the country,' Hoshi nodded, 'and let's admit that there are some foreigners who'd pay off old grudges on what did survive.'

'But then he'd have fought for nothing!' Mahoney protested.

'His sort would rather bring the whole works down than surrender to what they hate.' Hoshi said.

'A praiseworthy attitude when our side has it,' Fraser remarked with a sardonicism that was acrid in his mouth.

Hoshi regarded him out of narrowed slant eyes. 'What do you mean by that, Mark?'

'Nothing. Forget it.' Fraser stared out the port, at the ice and stars. 'We've got to fight him, of course,' he sighed.

'Yeah. I'm sure this speech of his will fetch in the outlier men that were doubtful when we talked to them earlier,' Hoshi said.

He began to pace up and down before the darkened screen, ticking his points off on work-roughened fingers. 'We can count on several hundred, at least. Their cats travel fast. We'll agree on several rendezvous points, and our sub-groups will move from them, converging in the eastern Sinus. With any luck, we can be at Aurora by eclipse time.'

'What will you fight with?' Mahoney challenged.

'We did pretty well in Shepard Pass, didn't we?' Tom Hoshi replied.

'Uh-huh,' his father said. 'Industrial equipment isn't too bad for close-in combat. We wouldn't have a chance against regular military forces. But the *Vega* people are Navy. They're short on small arms, and we outnumber them grossly. The ship can fire at us, but I don't think many guns can be brought to bear; and anyhow, those warheads are meant to explode inside other ships. Bursting in vacuum, they don't have much radius of destruction. We only need to get some sappers up to her. A few hundred pounds of tordenite, set off under the landing jacks, will put her quite out of action. Then we've got the whole bloody gang.'

'If they haven't lifted ship as soon as they saw us coming,' Fraser objected.

'They won't have a chance to. We can get over the horizon and up to the spacefield in half the time needed to raise a vessel that size, unless she's on full alert. Which she won't be, because that'd tie up too many of her crew for Swayne to get his production project started. Naturally, we've got to keep him from knowing about us beforehand. That shouldn't be hard. He can't tap light beams that aren't aimed at Aurora, and he hasn't the personnel to investigate the back country. Given a couple of weeks to get organised, he can send occasional patrols around to keep tabs on us. But we won't give him those weeks. If anyone radiophones while we're en route, those who stay behind can fob off questions.'

'Or tattle on us,' Colin said.

'Don't fear that,' Fraser assured him. 'The outliers are the really rambunctious individualists. Otherwise they'd have stayed in Aurora. But belay that "us", boy. You're staying here.'

'The hell I am!'

'The hell I am, *sir*.' Fraser rose too, and went to his wife.

She buried her face against him. 'Somebody's got to look after your mother and Ann, Colin. You're elected.'

And frankly, I envy you.

7

Tom Hoshi looked at the inertial locator dial on the controlboard, nodded, and stopped the cat. Its motor whirred to silence. 'We're here.'

Fraser checked the clock. 'None too soon, either,' he said. He wasn't sure if he spoke thickly or not. His head felt light, and his heart seemed about to burst through his ribs. But he calculated with habitual ease. 'Approximately three quarters of an hour for us, to Aurora; allow another fifteen minutes for snafu and extras – yeah, we'll get there shortly after eclipse, right about when we're supposed to.'

The five brothers crowded in with him seemed as unshakable as the father whose plan they were enacting. Fraser wondered if they were also scared down underneath. They snapped shut their faceplates and shrugged the loads of explosive over their shoulders, awkward bundles above the recycler tanks. Fraser waited till the last minute, when Tom was at the door, to close his own helmet. He didn't relish being locked in with himself.

Not waiting for the economy pump to finish its work, Tom opened the door as soon as pressure had dropped enough to allow it. Air puffed out in a frost-white cloud that expanded momentarily against rock and stars and then was gone. Fraser climbed through into blindness.

A wall rose before him, dizzily upward to a jagged rim. Half the sky was visible, because Dante Chasm is so wide that either edge lies below the horizon of the other. Jupiter could be seen, a thin gold crescent and the rest of the oblate disc a coalsack faintly rimmed with light. The sun was very near it. But crags and steeps threw their shadows from the east, over that place where the dozen cats had halted, so that night prevailed there and in the abyss below. Fraser could see nothing except bobbing blobs of undiffused light from the flashtubes, where men moved about and called to each other. Even given radar and a map of the way, he didn't understand how Tom had guided the caravan so far, without toppling over some brink to shatter in the deeps.

As if reading his mind, the driver snorted: 'Huh! Combat'll be a relief after that ride. I thought I was used to poking around in craters and rifts . . . till today.'

But it was one way of approaching undetected. Sam Hoshi counted on ground curvature to hide his army. The enemy might have patrols out, though. And men on foot, widely dispersed, would be a less profitable target than vehicles. They might even reach the *Vega* unseen, given a fight to distract the crew's attention.

Very nice and clear, Fraser thought in the hammering. *Sam makes a good general. What I don't quite get is why I, at my age, volunteered to go with this party. I do know spaceships better than average, I can tell where to put a demolition charge to do the most good, but I'm not the only one who can. Was it for Colin's sake? – I suppose I'm fighting for him and Ann more than for the United States or freedom or Eve, even. But I don't know. Those slogans seem pretty remote right now. God, how I wish I had a pill!*

Stim, euphoriac, all drugs, were in short supply, however, while Aurora remained in enemy hands. They must be saved for the wounded.

'Everybody set?' Tom's voice came to him as if from very far away. 'Up we go. Keep in Indian file, keep your light on the feet of the guy ahead.' He turned from the cat and began to climb.

Fraser scrambled immediately after. The stone was hard beneath his gauntlets, boots, and kneepieces. Uneroded, the slope had few loose rocks, and the weak gravity helped too, making the ascent less difficult than it looked. But he fumbled in murk, his breath rasped through his mouth, heat and sweat turned his suit into a steam bath. Now and then a radio curse leaped vividly at him. By the time he had emerged on top, his legs shook. He sat down and panted.

One by one, the bulky shapes appeared beside him. Thin harsh sunlight etched the faces in the helmets against a glittering sky, then drew darknesses under brow and nose and cheekbones until they seemed no more than sketches of men who crowded around. Tom counted off, stolidly. '. . . fifty-eight, fifty-nine, sixty, sixty-one. That's the lot of us. March.'

He started north across the blue-black lava plain. Nothing broke its bareness except the stipple of meteorite pocks, the ringwall of Dakota Crater, the distant sawtooth of the Glenns, and the men's own flying shadows. Fraser fell into the mile-eating rhythm – push with a foot, relax while you curved over the surface, strike with the other foot, feeling the global mass push back at you, continue on momentum until that leg was in position to shove . . .

Pat Mahoney drew alongside him, face a-grin. 'Some fun, hey, boss?'

Fraser had to clear his throat before he could say, 'Remind me to fire you for that, after the war's over.'

'Huh?' Mahoney's eyes probed him through the tricky light. 'Sorry. I didn't mean to be sophomoric. But still, this *is* fun. Beats the hell out of baseball.'

Fraser returned the look. 'Are you serious?'

'I always did like a scrap.'

Fraser had no reply. He'd outgrown such tastes thirty years ago. It came as a shock to him to realise, not from books but in the living and present flesh, that there were decent, kindly, civilised men who had not. *If 'outgrowing' is the right word. Maybe I'm the mistake of nature.*

Readiness to fight is a survival trait, I suppose. He worried the problem for some time. It was better than brooding on what was to come.

The sun slipped behind Jupiter. Night fell like a bomb. As eyes readapted, the plain changed from inkiness to a ghostly grey, and stars trod splendidly forth. The planet was a blank well among them, outlined in red where atmosphere refracted sunlight. The eclipse would last a little over three hours. Fraser wondered how Theor was doing. Had the dark gathered him up too? But memory refused to tell how Nyarr lay with relation to the sun at this time. Let's see, about twenty degrees north latitude – who cared, when they were almost at Aurora?

'There! The main radio mast!'

Fraser didn't recognise the voice that yelped in his earplugs. He squinted ahead and identified the shape, gaunt across the Milky Way. There was no sign or whisper or movement. He wondered sickly if Hoshi's other detachments had arrived yet.

'Okay,' said Tom, 'now we scatter. Keep about a hundred feet apart, maintain radio silence as long as possible, let me stay ahead – and run like the devil!'

They burst into speed. Foot-thrust sucked at Fraser's strength and wind impact jarred his teeth, his harsh breathing filled his ears. The destination didn't seem to come any nearer, he ran and ran across emptiness as a man runs in a nightmare ... and then in an instant Aurora lifted white before him, less than a mile away, with the topmost curve of the battleship's hull glimmering above, on the far side; and he saw the battle to the east.

The land seemed to crawl with gannycats, tiny beetle shapes that veered and darted, barely visible in the night. Shells burst among them, soundlessly blooming in fire; smoke and rock chips flew high each time in a cloud but settled quickly, so that while everything was in motion nothing seemed really to change. Now that he was over the horizon, his receiver screamed with voices:

'. . . here, this way, Tim!'

'Arnesen's squadron, deploy!'

'Steinmeier, get your men out on foot!'

'. . . goddammit, goddammit, goddammit –'

until the racket ceased to have meaning, became one with his pulse and pant and slamming footfalls. He switched his own transmitter back on. Under these conditions, it couldn't give him away to a detector. There was no longer time to be afraid. He had only a second in which to try to cherish the memory of Eve, and fail to conjure up her face; then he was too busy.

Tom Hoshi's band swung west, to approach the spaceport from an uncontested direction. As they neared Aurora, Fraser glimpsed men in the open, not far from the east side of town. They dashed about in ways that appeared merely Brownian. He wasn't sure whose side they were on. Both, perhaps. Swayne would likely have assigned such of his men as he could spare from operating the ship's guns and keeping the city dwellers corked up, to double as infantry with what small arms were available.

The buildings were now alongside, now behind. They hid the battle and cut off much of the radio noise. Fraser saw Tom turn at right angles and plunge toward the spacefield.

Something grabbed and threw him. He landed with a shock that smashed blackness through his head. A moment he lay in whirling and ringing. The world came back to him, he sat up and knew with vague amazement that he was alive. His skull throbbed and there was a hot salt trickle across his lips. But he lived.

Automatically he checked for an air leak. No sign of any. A craterlet had opened in the lava some yards away. Must have been a near miss by a shell, he thought in an impersonal fashion. The expanding gases had bowled him over, but done no serious harm. If the warhead had been designed to scatter shrapnel in a horizontal plane — but it was intended for use against ships and space stations. He got to his feet and bounded zigzag after the others. Pain touched his side. He ignored it.

Rock gave way to concrete. The *Olympia* loomed near an ugly and heavy outline in the half-light. *They saw us coming,* Fraser told himself, *but now we're inside the artillery's area of coverage.* The men had converged near the Jupiter vessel. Tom's voice slashed through: 'Go get 'er!'

They charged in a body at the battleship. She loomed before them big as the universe, the landing jacks like cathedral buttresses. But once the tordenite had been planted — there and there and there — and touched off, the giant must fall. Her own mass must crush the thin hull; and then a few more explosive sticks in the jets . . .

Fire pencilled from the shadows underneath. A colonist threw up his hands and flopped on his back. Another man died as he ran and crashed into the supports. The beams shot forth, again and yet again, until the dead lay in windrows with fog streaming from their pierced suits.

The charge broke and reeled away. Fraser found himself in retreat with Mahoney. They stopped at the *Olympia*. Fraser could only struggle for air, but Mahoney stood forth under the stars, waved and roared and drew men to him until a couple of score had rallied. Tom Hoshi was not among them. He must have fallen at the first barrage.

'Laser guns,' Mahoney snarled. 'They got a platoon under there, must've figured what we were up to — come on, we can still swamp the bastards.'

Someone stated an obscenity. 'You've got to get within a yard of a man before a torch'll burn him down. One of those guns'll pick you off before you're halfway.'

'We outnumber them,' Mahoney said.

'Not that much. Wait till the other guys have fought

through to the field. Then we'll outnumber them enough, maybe.'

'By heaven, I'll go myself, now, if you're too gutless!'

Fraser clamped a hand on Mahoney's arm. 'No, you don't,' he said. His breath had come back to him. And he noted that his mind was working again, with engineer precision and a cold commitment. 'We can't spare anybody for heroics. The only thing that matters is to get at that damned ship before she can blast off. Swayne saw at once what our intention is – well, that's obvious, but we didn't expect *he'd* expect an attack from this quarter. Maybe he didn't, exactly, but he did have the foresight to provide against one. So we can't do anything but wait till Sam Hoshi breaks through. Those few men below the ship have the fire power to stop us, but not to stop a hundred or more.'

'If Hoshi breaks through, you mean,' Mahoney said.

'Wait here and I'll go have a look,' Fraser offered.

He left the others and trotted north, past the parked moonships until he overlooked the battlefield. Slowly he interpreted the shadows and glints that flitted about out there. The cats and the men afoot had no clear formation that he could see. Shellbursts inhibited that. Wreckage and corpses lay scattered to show that the artillery fire had taken effect. But casualties seemed fairly light, as hoped, and the colonists were advancing by fits and starts toward the spacefield. One powerful assault . . .

A starburst rocket went up. Sam Hoshi's signal! Cats and men ceased dodging. The ether shook with an auroch's bellow. As one, the Ganymedeans poured forward.

Another shell flashed in the gloom. A vehicle rose in two pieces, strewing human shapes. But then Hoshi's van was inside the minimum range of the turrets – and the missile tubes weren't oriented right for . . .

Fraser pelted back. The darkling mass of his own group stirred beside the *Olympia*, broke into individuals and

63

clustered around. 'They're on their way,' he cried. 'A couple minutes more, and we can start.'

Aurora's buildings had cut off most of the radio racket. Now abruptly it became a hurricane. The ground trembled underfoot. Fire sheeted at the opposite end of the field. The main colonial force had won through.

'*Go*!' Mahoney yelled, and sprinted ahead.

Fraser followed, as near as he dared. Hit from two sides at once, the few men guarding the *Vega* could not but be overwhelmed. His hands fumbled at the packstraps.

The laser beams raked out. Air puffed from Mahoney's suit. He went to his knees. Another man leaped over him with a battle shout and was killed in midspring, fell with a terrible slowness and bounced when he struck.

Over and over the noiseless lightning spat. Instinct flung Fraser onto his belly. He raised his head and saw what looked like a wall of wrecked cats at the other end of the field. Guns were going off, energy casters and machine guns, improvised mines, to smash the colonial wave and hurl it back. Oh God, oh God, Swayne had not put more than the barest minimum of crew in ship and city, and none in the field. He had concentrated his force in emplacements dug out of the concrete; nobody had seen them in the wan starlight and Hoshi had charged into a man-mower.

Fraser tore the pack off his shoulders, crouched where he was, and ripped it open. The tordenite sticks spilled forth. He cursed out rage and grief in a stream while he twisted the three-minute detonator caps. But somehow through the clamour and the flashes he kept watch on the time, until the zero count was reached and he began lobbing them. One, two, three . . . they burst among the jacks, little glares of light and smoke. Maybe they injured a man or two. But hitting randomly, piecemeal, in vacuum, they did not, they could not harm a warcraft.

Something moved near Fraser. He looked dazedly

around and made out a shadow which bled freezing vapour. A fresh curtain of fire shone past the *Vega* and touched Pat Mahoney's face. With a torch in his arms, he crawled on his knees towards the ship.

The fire died down again. The ground no longer shook. Motion had ceased at the far side of the spacefield, all over the spacefield. The dead lay thick and the living were in flight. Fraser wormed to intercept Mahoney. 'Pat!' he called through what radio noise remained. 'Pat, come here, lemme get you safe.'

Mahoney kept crawling. Fraser threw his arms around him. The man's recycler tank dug painfully into his own bruised side. Mahoney struggled and damned him in a lunatic voice. 'Pat, don't throw yourself away, let's get out of here, get some help for you . . .'

'ATTENTION, INSURRECTIONISTS!'

The stars trembled with that sound. Mahoney stiffened, then sagged back into Fraser's embrace. Fraser lurched to his feet and began carrying the hurt man away. He was in easy shot of the *Vega*'s guardians, but he didn't care any more.

'ATTENTION, YOU GANYMEDEANS! THIS IS ADMIRAL SWAYNE.'

Must be using the main transmitter, broadcasting at full amplitude. So what? I've got to get Pat to a medic.

'YOU HAVE BEEN THROWN BACK IN TOTAL DEFEAT. ANY FURTHER ATTEMPTS WILL BE MET BY THE SAME FIREPOWER. YOU MAY PERHAPS HAVE SOME IDEA OF FORCING YOUR WAY INTO AURORA. DO NOT TRY. YOU WOULD ONLY SUCCEED IN WRECKING THE CITY. AND YOU WOULD KILL ITS CIVILIAN POPULATION. ALL OUTDOOR EQUIPMENT HAS BEEN SEQUESTERED. IF THE CITY IS BREACHED, EVERY MAN, WOMAN, AND CHILD IN THE

DAMAGED SECTION WILL DIE.'

Silence clapped down. It reached past the field and the plain, Ganymede and Jupiter, out to the whirlpool in Andromeda and beyond. Nothing lived but Fraser's rasping lungs and the blood that bubbled in Mahoney's gullet.

Then the Jehovah voice came back. 'ASSEMBLE BETWEEN THE CITY AND APACHE CRATER. IF YOU DO SO, YOU WILL NOT BE FIRED ON, WE ARE HOLDING OUR ARTILLERY FIRE UNTIL WE SEE WHETHER YOU OBEY THIS ORDER.'

There was no strength left in Fraser. He stumbled on somehow, past the moonships and around the junkyard where Hoshi's men had encountered Swayne's defence. The seepage from Mahoney's suit was less, pressure had dropped – *stop, slap a patch on, you idiot.*

'I AM PREPARED TO HOLD DISCUSSIONS WITH YOUR LEADERS, PROVIDED YOU WAIT AT THE DESIGNATED PLACE. MEANWHILE YOU MUST ADMIT THAT YOU ARE BEATEN. THE *VEGA* CAN BE READY TO LIFT WITH A SMALL CREW IN LESS THAN ANOTHER HOUR. YOU CANNOT GET ONTO THE SPACEFIELD IN A YEAR. ACCEPT YOUR DEFEAT, GANYMEDEANS.'

Fraser laid Mahoney down, squatted beside him and hunted in his repair kit. Another pause came, a stillness so absolute that he heard the hiss of cosmic radio interference in his earplugs. He bent close, trying to see if Mahoney moved. Eyes stared back at him, full of reflected starlight. A froth of blood had formed on the mouth and around the nostrils. Nothing disturbed it. Fraser held his breath and listened for the other man's. All he heard was the seething between the galaxies.

8

West over sea, on the foggy edge of sight, lifted the shimmering cliffs of the Orgover Islands. Theor could just discern the surf that battered their feet, the waves and maelstroms that dashed between them. More clearly there came to him the sound, like an endless thunderstorm, brimming the red-tinged bowl of the sky. The ship had not been built which could live in those tide-rips and cross-currents. But the islands sheltered the stretch between themselves and the mainland, so that Nyarr's fleet walked over placid grey ammonia and the black sands of Gillen Beach were lapped by mere ripples. Beyond, pastureland slanted eastward and southward until it lost itself in distance. The Steeps of Jonnary walled off the north.

Theor gazed at the looted ruin of a fisher town, the fifteen or more octads of lean dark ships lying at anchor, the army of giants ashore who swarmed into formation as his own folk approached. Signal drums were sounding on both sides, through the ocean tumult, rapid thutter from the Nyarran ranks and a slower bass boom that called to the Ulunt-Khazul. Spearheads flashed high among banners, above the hordes.

Elkor scowled. 'They aren't manning their ships,' he said. 'They're keeping almost entirely on land.'

Norlak's slim hands twisted together. 'Can our levies face so many? We counted on dividing the opposition.'

'Once we attack their fleet ...' Theor's voice faded. Obviously the Ulunt-Khazul knew better than to go aboard then.

67

Elkor made a headshake shrug. 'Having come to live in Medalon, they may as well sacrifice the ships,' he interpreted.

'No, that makes no sense,' Norlak said. 'Even if they are resolved on victory or death, well, they have to bring the rest of their people sometime.'

'They must be counting on building more vessels after the conquest, or using ours,' Elkor decided. He paced restlessly, around and around the foredeck. 'This is a blow to our plans,' he muttered. 'We've committed so many folk to the fleet that the enemy land force – allowing for them being superior warriors individually – may very well defeat our troops. Perhaps we should land here and now ... No. It would take too long. They'd be upon us before we straightened the confusion.'

He stood a while pondering. A breeze came; he lifted his massive head and announced: 'We'll carry on as planned, get in among their ships, cut down what few enemy people are aboard and then make our landing. That way, they'll be taken in the rear while still engaging our ground forces. Umfokaer, have a forgarman so inform Guard Chief Walfilo. Tell him to hold firm at every cost, for we'll come to his help quite fast.'

The officer saluted and called to the signaller. 'We'd best get ready,' Norlak said.

'Aye.' They began to equip themselves. The ship, the whole fleet crawled with folk doing likewise.

Theor squirmed into the kannik-skin mailcoat that protected his body; the similar jacket for his torso; the solid plates hung loosely above the vulnerable openings for gills and vents; the peaked helmet; the round shield for his left arm; the belt of knives. His right hand hefted an axe. The gear was unexpectedly heavy, and it was annoying to feel his crest cramped. He tried to convince himself that combat against invaders was no worse than against an enraged

68

snouthorn. But he couldn't believe it. The wrongness of the day, the *disorientation,* hit him. He looked at his male demi-father's face and read only sternness. Norlak's jitters were almost a comfort, making him feel less alone.

Drums crashed. The Ulunt-Khazul infantry formed up and started toward the Nyarrans. Their spears rippled like a forest in the wind.

Theor plucked his attention away, back seaward. The enemy fleet was still a couple of miles off, but he could observe details. They were lapstrake craft, shorter and with less beam than his galleys, entirely decked over. The absence of figureheads gave them a dauntingly businesslike look. But what was that framework jutting from each prow? And without sidewheels or masts or even oar ports, how did they move?

A few figures bustled about on them, in helmets and hornplate cuirasses that flung back the light as if metallic. Several boats were moving out into deeper water. Unlike Nyarran auxiliary craft, round coracles sculled by a single person, these were narrow, with outriggers and lateen sails. 'Where are they going?' Theor wondered aloud. 'What are they about?'

'Nothing good for us,' Norlak said.

'Their vessels are not equipped to ram, as we already knew,' Elkor said. He had counted originally on sinking them thus before their crews could grapple fast and board his own ships. 'But they may well be faster than us. Could they intend simply to flee for safety?'

'If so,' Theor forced himself to remark, 'we can make our landing still the sooner.'

'I don't like this,' Norlak mumbled. His antennae twitched. 'The air stinks with ill-omen.'

The Nyarran ships plodded on. There was no more chanting from the wells: only shuffle and creak, the coxswain's count, the thresh of the wheels overside. Males lined the deck above, shifting their weapons from hand to hand, staring ahead. Theor glanced at the shore. The two armies had changed from a walk to a jog trot; their banners bobbed against low stawr clouds in the east.

'Ulloala! What's that?' exclaimed Elkor.

Theor whirled about and followed the pointing spear. The enemy sailboats had halted at the edge of a large sea pasture. Their pilots cupped hands about throat pouches and shouted. The call wailed to Theor through the Orgover thunders and drumplay ashore. The weed surface broke open, waves boiled outward, shape after huge black shape rose until the whole strait seemed covered with them.

Norlak reared and gibbered. 'What *are* they?'

The muscles bunched around Elkor's jaws. 'Ocean beasts. I've never seen or heard of their kind, but – Domesticated. So that's what pulls their ships!'

The archbacked forms vibrated tails and flippers and darted toward the Ulunt-Khazul vessels. Sailors poised on the framework at every bow, harnesses in hand. Someone yelled, aft of Theor; a groan rose from Nyarr's fleet.

Elkor stood fast and estimated. 'About half as long as a galley, those creatures,' he said, 'and almost as massive, I'm sure. I don't know what they can do to us, but plainly the enemy is counting on them. That's why he could afford to concentrate his strength on land.' He brought the butt of his spear down on the planks. 'We must assume he knows his own capabilities. I dare no longer meet him at sea. But we can beach before he's ready to fight. That harnessing must be a slow operation.'

'Beach? Here?' Theor protested. 'Demi-father, I've fished along Gillen. The drop-off isn't steep enough at this point. We'll smash our side-wheels in the shallows.'

'They can be repaired,' Elkor snapped. 'Death can't.' He scanned the ground, 'if we make for yonder spit, Walfilo's band should have passed it by the time we arrive. We'll group while he holds off the enemy, and join him from

70

behind. It's not as good as striking the Ulunt-Khazul rear, but it will have to do. Send the message, Umfokaer.'

'Aye, aye.' The officer gestured to the signaller below, who unfurled the flag he carried. The nearest forgar came down. Umfokaer shouted to the rider, who rose and repeated the words to his hovering fellows. They scattered the command over the fleet.

Theor gripped the stempost and stared out at the enemy.

The sea beasts neared the Ulunt-Khazul ships. A nude sailor went over each side, struck with a splash, and swam forward. An animal stopped for him. He climbed up onto the shoulders, behind the long neck, straddled with four legs, and waved. His mates flung the ends of harness at him. He caught them and went to work.

Nyarr's ships had scarcely changed course when the Ulunt-Khazul fleet was in motion. They came in a blunt wedge, ammonia foaming white where tails churned and again where the sharp bows cut through. The riders were all but hidden in spray. But the heads of their mounts reared above, gaunt and gape-jawed.

Elkor joined Theor, laid a hand on his son's shoulder and said most gently: 'So I was wrong about that too. They'll catch us a mile from safety. Well . . . if we don't outlive this day . . . you were a welcome guest.'

Theor bent his head. They do not weep on Jupiter.

Norlak shook his dirk aloft. Once the irrevocable had happened, a demimale's terrors usually left him. 'Let them come and be eaten!' he yelled. Some of the crew shouted him an answer. Most were silent, clutching the rails and their weapons, waiting.

'Organise a defence at this end,' Elkor said. 'I'd best be aft with the steersmale. Fight well – no, I know you will.' He turned and went quickly down the gangway.

The armies ashore laid spears in rest and broke into a gallop.

As Theor helped Norlak deploy three octads of pike

wielders on the foredeck, his hunter's hearts rallied within him. Animals could be faced! Terrifying though they looked, those beasts weren't going to ram – not unless they wanted to break their necks. They would probably lay alongside and try to snatch crewfolk off the deck. A wall of shields and a hedge of spears would meet them. He called his orders out. With a growl and a rattle, the Nyarrans locked ranks.

Closer, now ... Theor raised his axe. If any fangs got near him, he thought he could chop the jawbone loose. He glared into the eyes of the closest oncoming beast and braced his feet on the deck. Behind him, spearbutts grounded with a solid *thunk*.

The monster veered to port. Spray whirled as its flippers backed ammonia. The rider tugged at the horns of the collar. The beast rolled around. Its tail smashed out.

The ship staggered. Wood cracked across, splinters hailed, the line at the rail was broken and two Nyarrans shrieked in agony. Another blow, and another – They weren't carnivores, they weren't going to bite, they crushed!

Forgars swooped low. The riders stabbed with futile lances. The sea beast shook its head and went beneath. Its controller stayed on its back.

The creature rose again by the paddlewheel and broke that to pieces with sheer mass. The crippled ship wallowed in the waves. Once more the beast sounded. It couldn't go deep without dragging down the vessel it pulled. But it got under the Nyarran keel.

The well erupted treadmill walkers. A gush of ammonia followed them. The ship lurched and began to sink.

'Board the enemy!' Elkor shouted above the rush and trample. There was no way to do so. The beast had withdrawn. Across yards, Theor saw how it grinned, how the invaders howled and brandished their weapons. He looked over his fleet and saw it breaking up, ships foundering, ships fleeing, the sea power of Nyarr become flotsam.

He scrambled frantically out of his armour. The deck tilted, crewfolk slid toward the incoming sea, their cries overrode the surf and the clangour on shore. Theor wrapped a leg around the stempost and clung fast. He had a glimpse of Norlak tumbling off, dragged under by his own heavy gear. Then he had stripped, save for the knife belt that he put on again. He dived.

The impact, under Jovian gravity, was savage. Whirl and turmoil followed, until he re-emerged and struck out for land.

Other heads bobbed about. He recognised Elkor in the swarm and moved that way. The ship turned as she settled, the stern lifted. With one liquid roar, she plunged to the bottom.

'Here!' Elkor called. 'To me, Nyarr!'

As if in answer, a sea beast arrived. Flukes and flippers pounded about among the swimmers. The foam that flew up was blood colour. The Nyarrans died with their Reeve, and the Ulunt-Khazul laughed aloud.

Theor raised his torso high, gills wide open to get as much air as he could. The monster searched around for more prey. He went below.

Dim, tawny light enclosed him, and a bitter smell-taste of dissolved hydrocarbons. Currents fluttered around his skin. He swam until his head rocked from lack of air. Finally he must surface.

The butchery was continuing. He seemed to be well away, himself. There was no time for horror. His legs pumped, driving him toward the beach.

'Hungn rogh mamlun!'

Theor looked behind. An Ulunt-Khazul warrior swam after him. The webbed feet and the long tail pushed the grey body at thrice his own speed. A knife glistened in one hand. The face was akindle with anticipation.

Theor drew a dagger of his own. *So he wants a little personal amusement? I'll give him some.* More coolly than a human could have done, he calculated his actions. He was no match for his enemy as a swimmer, but . . .

The Ulunt-Khazul dived. *Going to rip me from beneath, I see.* Theor put his head down while treading ammonia. The shadowy shape sped upward at him. He folded his legs under his stomach and sank. The knife flashed past. His free hand snatched, clamped onto the weapon wrist.

His opponent blocked his own stab and got a grip on that arm. They tumbled over and over, down through the sea together. Theor wrapped his front legs around the great body. The claws on his hind feet went against the abdomen. He rowelled.

Down and down! Was the ocean filling with blood, or was that his own faintness? His hearts were about to burst, He felt his captured hand forced back, his own clasp loosening. He thought of Norlak and Elkor and raked with all his power. Something ripped.

Suddenly his dagger hand was free. With a head loaded with thunder, he continued to hang on and disembowel. Nothing but a loss of consciousness stopped him. He never knew afterward how he regained the surface.

Slowly his brain got function back. There was no sense of victory in him, only a resolve to reach the shallows before his last strength went.

The distance was still considerable. He shook the wetness from his eyes and peered ahead.

The beach was one boiling of combat. He heard screams, axes hammering on shields, feet trampling the fallen and slipping in blood. But half the banners of Nyarr were down. Those of Ulunt-Khazul pressed ever deeper into the fray. 'I'm coming!' he called, and damned his thews for their exhaustion.

He had not arrived when the striped flag of Walfilo pulled

free. The Nyarrans streamed after it, still keeping a semblance of order, their rearguard smiting and stabbing. Forgars were thick in the riven air overhead. The riders hurled darts and stones, grey giants went to earth, the Ulunt-Khazul attack was blunted.

Drums boomed. A corps of invaders broke from the main battle and made for the Nyarran baggage train. Few were there to resist them. They swarmed through and possessed it.

Walfilo's remnant hastened northward, toward the Steeps of Jonnary. They had no other way to go. Everywhere else the Ulunt-Khazul ramped, bounding after stragglers and hewing them down. *We saved something*, Theor thought, *but for what?*

His feet touched bottom. He stood and shuddered.

Eventually a measure of will rose in him. The enemy weren't pressing the pursuit. It wasn't worth their while. Still numerous, and with a cadre of professionals, Walfilo's followers could exact a heavy toll if forced to make a last-ditch stand. Better for Chalkhiz to let them flee, beaten and supplyless; let the wilderness complete their destruction.

I've got to join them.

Theor waded to the beach and started off. He must thread a path among hideously battered dead and wounded. The sound of pain wove in and out of the surf-noise. 'Drink,' pleaded a demimale he remembered. 'Theor, is that you, give me a drink!' A spear had transfixed the body.

Theor could not help himself. He bent to take the uplifted hands between his own. 'I have nothing,' he said. 'Farewell.'

'Don't go, Don't leave me here alone.'

The son of the Reeve started off to do whatever he could to help. A shadow fell across him. Two Ulunt-Khazul had their pikes aimed at his thorax.

One of them made a gesture: Come.

9

Even before its short term was over, the day drew to a close. For a strong wind sprang up from the south, driving a roof of black sulphurous-edged clouds over the sky. Lightning glared ever oftener among them, thunder rolled through the droning air, the distant surf and the waves now loud in the strait. They were bio-luminescent, those waves, they reached a tattered sheet of icy glow out beyond the hunch-backed islands and spouted sparks where they struck the beach. The Ulunt-Khazul drew their ships and boats ashore, huddled in groups and muttered to each other.

Such few Nyarrans as had been captured stood silent in their misery. Theor was roused from a doze when a pair of warriors came and spoke to the guards. Their language cut rough through the weather. A halberd pointed to him. The new arrivals prodded him into motion. He walked slowly, stumbled on hobbled feet, up the strand toward the booths that had been erected for the chieftains. His wrists were tied together, but in front of him, so that he could still reach the communicator hung around his neck. Doubtless a super-stitious unease had saved it from being taken off him. Once again he pressed the button. 'Mark,' he whispered. 'Anyone. I am in need.' There was still no answer.

A spear point urged him through the entrance to the largest booth. Chalkhiz stood within, arms enfolded. A light-flower cast feeble rays from above, leaving his coarse face mostly in darkness; but the eyes glittered like the weapons stacked against one trembling wall.

'Good evening,' he said with a grin.

76

Theor had no response.

'Would you like refreshment?' Chalkhis waved at a bowl of ammonia and a platter of fish on a bench. Theor recognised a taunt, but his upbringing was too practical for pride to stand in the way. He accepted ravenously.

'It is good that you survived, and that a male who had been with my delegation noticed you among the prisoners.' Chalkhiz said. 'Perhaps we can make a bargain.'

'What have I to bargain with?' Theor asked wearily.

'Not much,' Chalkhiz agreed. 'Still, Nyarr town has strong defences.'

'It will cost you dearly to take,' Theor said. 'When word comes with those who escaped southward, every male and demimale who was not here today – and they are many, because of the ranching season – will go there with wife and young, to make a stand.'

'No doubt. Otherwise we could destroy them one at a time. But an agreement might yet be reached.'

Theor's control broke in two. 'With animals like your-selves?'

Chalkhiz snatched for an axe, withdrew his hand, and said in anger: 'We take what is ours by right. Had your lands been flooded, storm-beaten, ruined, the fish deserting, your people starving, you would try to win a country elsewhere. Would you not?'

I suppose so, it sighed in Theor. *But I'll not admit that to him.*

A gust struck the booth so that the planks groaned. Rain could be heard marching closer.

'Well,' Chalkhiz leaned forward. 'I did not bring you here to trade insults, but to talk. I gather your he-parents have both died.' The memory came back to strangle Theor. 'If I understand your laws aright, this makes you the new Reeve. Your folk ought to obey if you call on them to surrender.'

'No. We are a free people. They need not heed me. And I

77

hope they wouldn't. Not that I would ever speak such words.'

'Listen to me. If they fight, we will destroy them utterly. But if they give up, we will let them go beyond the mountains. That's not a good country, I know, but they would at least be alive.'

Theor's fingers wrestled with each other. 'No.'

'Think well. Your land cannot be that dear to you.'

'You had only some wretched swamps and islands, did you not? We built here for more sixty-fours of years than our records run back. Dams, dikes, cleared fields, houses, everything we have is drenched with the blood and toil of our ancestors. You do not understand what it means.'

'To you perhaps. Your kin-tree have led that effort for so long. But to every last person in Nyarr? I doubt it.'

Theor struggled to hold himself expressionless. The guess had struck too shrewdly.

'How could we trust you not to fall on us once we had opened the passages through the city hedge?' he countered.

Chalkhiz laughed. 'You would have to take my promise. However, we are fewer than you, and less skilled in land maintenance. When we inherit the country, we also inherit the hungry barbarians of the north. Are we likely to spend troops on a large, armed mass of Nyarrans without provocation?' Grimly: 'I can promise that if you do not yield, there will be nothing but death or enslavement for your people.'

Theor summoned what strength remained to him. 'The core of our army got away today,' he said. 'It can return, and can be reinforced. You will be the ones destroyed, unless you are the ones who go settle in Rollarik.'

Chalkhiz made a spitting noise. Thunder banged overhead.

After a while, the Ulunt-Khazuli said: 'I shall have you kept apart from the others. We will be here for a few days yet making ready to march on Nyarr. I advise you to think hard about this matter, and to change your mind. Otherwise we will cut you to pieces and eat you before the city hedge.' He shouted out the doorway. A guard looked in. Chalkhiz spoke an order and turned his back.

The warrior's hand closed on Theor's arm and guided him away. They walked for some distance along the strand, to the edge of camp. A small booth stood there. The guard pushed his prisoner through and took up a position outside the open entrance. Lightning covered the sky, etching him black against the hasty clouds and blazing off the head of his pike.

Thunder followed, and the first rain roared on the shelter. Theor locked his knees to rest in night and racket. For a moment he was maliciously pleased – let that fellow stand out in the wet!

Despair rolled over him. What could he do? What could anyone do? The invaders were victorious. Norlak the clever and Elkor the unbendable lay under the sea, and the Ulunt-Khazul had butchered Nyarr's fallen for meat. They could ring the city and starve its defenders while their legions plundered the countryside. Might it not be best to yield . . . forsake the land, forsake identity, slink off toward barbarism in the wilderness? A shabby freedom: but worse would be to become cattle for the conquerors. He thought of the child Leenant carried, his and hers and gentle Pors', cringing before an owner.

'Theor!'

He started. The blood ran through him louder than the gale outside.

'Theor, this is Mark. Do you receive me?'

He brought the disc to his throat, but could not hold it steady. 'Most yes,' he stammered.

Another flash in the sky showed his sentry. Rain rushed off his flanks. He had not stirred. In so much wind and wave-beat, the little sound muffled in Theor's hands did not reach him.

'I've been . . . busy. This is my first chance at a transmitter linked with JoCom's. How are you?'

Theor told his story in a few flat words.

'Oh God damn everything,' said Fraser beyond the lightning.

'What has happened to you, mind-brother?'

The air had grown cold, and was damp in Theor's gills. He recalled what he had once been told by Fraser, that Ganymede was so chill that ammonia itself lay frozen. Jupiter's atmosphere trapped heat . . . but tonight the heat seemed to be bleeding away, back toward those dead globes that rolled through outer space. He shivered.

'Theor, I'm so unspeakably sorry about you . . . Uh, me.' A bleak chuckle. 'Better off, but also beaten. They stopped our attack on Aurora and threw us back. Now we're camped at the place they ordered, and their leaders are about to open talks with ours.'

'Ill is this time. Has the whole universe gone awry? But tell me, if your foes have so much power, why do they negotiate at all?'

Perhaps there is a clue buried in that to what I should do about my own enemy's wish.

'Well, we'd be hard to wipe out. And, of course, if driven to desperation, we might wreck the city. We wouldn't actually, but I suspect Swayne credits us with a touch of his own fanaticism. He needs its facilities for his scheme. So he'll try for some compromise, such as returning home without any further punishment.'

'Have you any hope of striking again, successfully? Or at least of summoning help from Earth?'

The sand was chill and moist beneath Theor's pads. He rubbed his feet one by one against his legs.

Fraser sighed. 'I don't see how. Even if we could get hold

of a moonship, none is equipped to go beyond the Jovian System. That is, they could, but they'd be unable to accelerate long enough to build up the speed for a hyperbolic orbit. The trip would take many months. We haven't got much time before Swayne returns home.'

'Be cheered,' said Theor clumsily. 'At worst, you will still live in your own land, and even if you do not like your masters, they will be of your own kind.'

Lightning flashed anew. The thunder rolled for minutes, shaking the ground.

'Whereas you – Theor, we've got to get you out of there.'

'How?'

Despite all hopelessness, the Jovian's pulses jumped. They had so many marvels in the sky; could there possibly be one for him?

'Describe your situation as carefully as you're able.'

Theor did so. When he had finished, the transmission time stretched till he thought it must break.

'Hm. You're not very near anyone else, and you've got a storm for cover. That's something. Could you overcome your guard?'

'I am hobbled and my hands are bound. He has a pike and dagger.'

The answer flashed into Theor even as he waited.

Fraser spoke it: 'If you could distract his attention, you might be able to grab one of those weapons. Eh? Dangerous as hell, but you don't have anything in particular to lose. Turn up your communicator to full volume and throw it out when he isn't looking. I'll yell.'

'Aye!' Theor pulled the cord of the disc over his head.

Fraser hesitated. 'If you get hurt, though –'

'As you say, that makes small difference to my present plight. Hurgh ... let me think ...' Calm descended upon him as he stood. 'Yes, I would do best to steal a boat. They could track me over this wet ground. and they can run

81

faster than I. In the past I have had some experience with sail, and you can also advise me. Very well, when you hear me call aloud, speak for a few moments. Imitate a Jovian voice as well as possible – though it will still sound impressively alien. I have a feeling that night makes these Ulunt-Khazul nervous anyway.'

He paused, wondering how to frame a farewell. Before long he might lie with a blade of whetted ice alloy between his ribs.

'If it made any sense for me, I'd say God be with you, Theor. Good luck, anyhow.' Fraser's voice wavered. 'Yeah. All the luck in the universe.'

'No keep some for yourself. Now wait for my call. Good-bye, mind-brother.'

Theor advanced to the doorway, the disc hidden between his palms. He stuck his head out. Rain flung against his brows and runnelled down his crest. The guard, a bulk in the flicker-touched gloom, very faintly glowing by his own infrared radiation, growled an order at him and jabbed with the pike.

Theor pointed with his arms and exclaimed.

The guard looked in that direction, only for a split second, but there was time for Theor to toss the communicator a little way to his other side. Now came the transmission lag – the warrior scowled back at him and poised his shaft. No doubt he was saying, 'Get inside before I skewer you.'

The disc wailed.

The Ulunt-Khazuli leaped in the air. Fraser's words snarled at him. Lightning ignited; briefly the beach lay under ruthless white illumination, so that Theor could see the guard's sheathed knife, the rivets on his pike and a scar on his cheek. Dazzlingly to Jovian eyes, the disc reflected that glare.

The guard jabbed wildly at it. His mouth gaped with

terror and his throat worked with shouts for help. Theor was forgotten. As thunder came to drown out both voices, the Nyarran lurched forward.

His hands closed on the knife. The Ulunt-Khazuli swung toward him. Theor drew the blade and stabbed under the great jaws.

Arms closed around his torso. Pain lanced as his gills were bruised. He haggled the knife in an arc. Blood spurted into his face. The clutch on him slipped away. The guard went to the ground, cried out once more, flopped like a landed fish, and died.

Now only the wan shimmer in the sky gave light, continuous electric discharges in the upper atmosphere whose radiation filtered down through many cloud layers. The sea, the camp, the land were locked away in rain. Theor said aloud: 'I have him, Mark. Keep silence. I can only hope that no one heard the fight.' He caught the pike awkwardly between his foreknees and sawed the bonds on his wrists across the edged head. It kept slipping sideways and cutting him. Rain beat his body, wind skirled, the sea stamped.

Free! He withdrew the knife from the guard's throat and slashed away the hobbles on his legs. Next . . . best take the belt and sheath. The body was heavy to roll over. He got the belt around himself, the communicator back under his head, picked up the guard's pike and started for the beach.

Lightning turned the world incandescent again. Theor saw two Ulunt-Khazul approaching. They must be on their way by mere unlucky chance, for they were in no hurry. But the axes on their shoulders shone through the rain.

Darkness and thunder. Theor ran.

The boats lay on the beach, not far off, anchors biting the ground. Half blind, Theor strained against one prow. No . . . no movement . . . he'd have to flee on foot, then. By wading through the shallows he could prevent tracks, but it would be deadly slow . . . The hull stirred and grated down the sandslope. He flung the anchor and pike aboard and gave himself to the task.

Each time the lightning came, he thought surely he must have been seen. Confusion was loose in the camp, warriors galloping back and forth, shouting as they ran. The dead guard had been found but probably no one except Chalkhiz knew he'd been watching a prisoner, so ... Ammonia splashed about Theor's hocks. The boat came afloat. He pulled himself into the open hull and lay shaking.

No. He mustn't. He had to be away. He picked himself up and groped aft to the mast. The sail was furled around the yard, an unfamiliar arrangement of lines and grommets baffled him. But at least there was some light here, from the sea.

Slowly he puzzled out what he must do. The boat rose and fell, rocked and yawed in the waves. Drifting north before the wind, though; that was something. Theor undid the last lashing and pulled on the halyard. The sail cracked like thunder and threshed up. Theor made fast. The sail filled and the boat plunged its nose into a wave. Spray sheeted cold and flaming across him. He let down the dagger-board and crawled on to the tiller.

Now ... straighten her out ... fill the sail with wind ... drive her!

The vessel heeled. Billows rose with a volcanic noise under the hissing strakes, climbed and climbed, broke in a flurry that spouted into the hull. And rain came from aft, to smack against bellying sail and thrumming rig, to pour down between the thwarts. He'd have to bail. There was a notched semicircle below the tiller, to lock the rudder in place. Good trick, that, he thought, and crawled along the pitching length in search of a container.

Finding a bucket, he worked busily. He was anxious to get back and steer. The boat needed close control in this much weather. He had nearly finished when another lightning stroke came, at a moment when his head chanced to be up and his eyes turned back along his course.

Land was already lost in the dark. But a black, long-necked shape could be seen, distance-dwindled, yet growing as it closed the gap. Frigid fire boiled in its wake. The hope drained out of Theor.

10

'Mark,' he said. 'Are you there yet?'

He returned to the tiller, unlocked it, and brought the bucking craft to heel.

'Yes, of course I am,' Fraser's voice said in the rushing of rain and sea. 'Are you okay? You got clear?'

'I did. But I fear this will be the last time we speak together. They must have seen my boat. A great swimming animal is in pursuit, with a rider – the kind of animal that smashed our fleet. I cannot outrun it, and will not surrender.' Theor uttered his equivalent of a sigh. 'Live gladly. May your cause prosper.'

He peered aft, into the rain that beat against his nictitating membranes. Only one creature was plunging through the ammonia. Well, that was quite sufficient.

'What?' Fraser cried. 'No! Couldn't you get ashore ahead of it?'

'Not at the rate it is nearing me.'

While he crouched and awaited a reply, Theor looked to starboard. The shore was still invisible, even when lightning struck. He debated setting the rudder again, going over the side and trying to swim. But he'd never survive that stretch, as rough as it had become.

Fraser cursed in anguish. 'I'd give my right arm to send you a gun you could use! Haven't you any weapon?'

'A knife and a long pike –' What he might do exploded in Theor. 'Hold! I have a thought. Wild indeed, but the least chance is better than none. Wait for my word.'

Again he made his way forward. His hand closed on the

86

pike and he thrust it ahead of him, bracing it against a rib to jut out over the prow. The anchor helped weigh down the butt, and he passed the rope many times around the shaft before securing it to the thwarts. That was slow work, in darkness and wet, in pitching and rolling. By the time he had finished and got back to the tiller, the monster was appallingly near.

'Mark!' he called. 'Now I need your counsel. You said to me erstwhiles that you have sailed the seas of Earth. I have less experience. Can I get upwind of my follower?' Fear had left him with the prospect of action, and he described methodically what he planned to do and how the boat was rigged.

The same steadiness took over in Fraser. He explained how to come about and beat into the wind. Theor took the sheets in his hands, held the tiller with one foot, and put the helm over. The boat swung heavily, canted so far that the outrigger dipped below the surface, righted itself and went crabwise on the tack.

The monster veered. Theor clung doggedly to his course. Ammonia swirled about his ankles in cold scintillating currents; spray mingled with rain to windward and pounded over his head. He passed not far from his pursuer, so close that he saw another lightning flash reflected in an eye. The Ulunt-Khazuli astride its shoulders hauled on the collar horns. Sea churned about tail and flippers. Then the enemy was behind.

Fraser's rapid instructions cut through the storm. Theor came about onto the other tack. The monster slowed to rearward. 'I think he thinks I am giving up and heading back to captivity,' Theor said. 'Good, that is as I hoped.'

He let the distance grow a little more. The boat fought him. All at once he put the helm up and wore ship. After an instant of battle, he was again running downwind, straight toward the beast.

If only the rider does not see the spearhead — Fraser's encouragement was small company.

The black breast rose sheer before him. He struck. The pike went home.

The shock threw him to the boards. He heard a whistling scream. The monster recoiled, swung around, heaved the boat in an arc through the waves that brawled over the rail. Theor looked up and saw the bony head etched against heaven.

The beast sounded. The bows went under. Theor tumbled forward, crashed into a thwart and splintered it. Through night and clamour he thought, *Well anyhow, I shall take that thing and its rider to the bottom with me!*

Stempost and pikeshaft broke. The boat lurched up again. A filled hull dragged at a still floating outrigger, the mast rocked above an ensemble lying awash. Theor clung battered and half blind to the rail. Waves burst across him.

Somehow the rigging stayed put. Wind shoved at the sail and the wreck stumbled onward, north through the strait.

A glance, beyond curtains of wet flame — The beast shot aloft, broke its full length into the air, a tormented arc that ended in a geyser. There was no trace of the Ulunt-Khazuli. The monster broached again, ten feet to starboard. The tail flukes lifted, smashed down, timber shattered and the boat went to pieces. In another crazed splash, the animal vanished.

Theor's limbs threshed. His head came to the surface, his upper gills drank the wild air. A wave broke over him, he sank stunned. His last consciousness observed that he was still trying to swim.

Something rammed his flank. He closed arms and legs around it in simple automatism. For ages he clung there . . .

Was not the weather abating?

The rain slacked off, became a drizzle and finally a thick, blowing fog. The gale turned into the slow, ponderous thrust

88

of a normal Jovian wind. The sea still marched loud and high, and a current had seized on Theor's bit of flotsam. But he could keep himself unsubmerged now, he need not fight for his grip, and gradually the daze cleared out of his brain.

He stared about. The fog shut off his vision after a yard or two, but being full of spray suspended in the thick air, it glowed like the sea. He lived in a roil of light through which resounded the hollow clashing of waves. He rocked up and down, rolled from side to side, with a swing that grew steadily longer and easier. He was too tired, too aching in every cell, to feel more than a vague wonder at being alive. But he examined his carrier with a shred of hope.

It was the outrigger, still attached to the upper strake and some fragments of rib. That was a lucky combination, fairly stable as long as Theor held himself low. Braced against the joining struts, he could even relax. Some cordage had got snarled around the bit timber, and several bits of wood were caught in it, including half a thwart that could be used as a paddle.

I might live yet, he realised, and brought the communciator to his mouth. 'Mark!'

Something hooted, far out in the liquid smoke.

'Ugh – uh – Theor?'

'Myself.' He achieved a smile. 'Are you surprised? I am!'

As life crept back into him, he noticed hunger. Thirst was no problem, the mineral content of sea ammonia being too slight to matter. There was even a bit of nourishment in it. Organic materials, such as amino acids, were formed in the upper atmosphere, where sunlight irradiated gases like methane and ammonia. They tended to settle and thus go below the level where ultraviolet light could break them up again. Such of these molecules as reached the oceans supported a microbial population, which higher animals could digest. But the concentration, in this energy-poor environment, was too low to help much. It had been long since Theor enjoyed Chalkhiz's scornful hospitality.

'Yes, surprised and mighty damn glad! I fell asleep, sitting by the transceiver here. Or rather, my body did, the traitor. How are you?'

Theor explained. 'After I get ashore,' he finished, 'I may be able to find Walfilo's people. They must have crossed the Steeps of Jonnary, which I must now be north of myself.'

Though that is a big and wild country, nearly unknown. Old ones tell that the Hidden Folk dwell in those untrodden mountains which cut it off from the sea.

'Well ... I feel so bloody helpless, Theor. I can't even stay by the radio much longer. In these past hours, while you were drifting half asleep, I've already had to go to a conference, and now ... uh, I have to see someone. She says it's important. I don't know what'll happen, and I may not have access to a transceiver for a spell.'

'Call me when you can. Good fortune to you, mind-brother.'

The loneliness closed in again.

Day brought a slight brightening, but otherwise Theor remained in a formlessness that glimmered. Not until afternoon did the fog break up, in tatters and immense whirling banks. When he saw land he cried out.

He had come far indeed. The sheltering Orgover archipelago was behind him, and he drifted a couple of miles from unbroken cliffs of black ice. Their tops were hidden by the low mist; he could only guess at the height. Driven by the largest moons, surf crashed in a murderous white smother along the narrow beaches at their feet. The boom came to him across dark choppy waves, until he felt it in his bones. Had he not been so beaten and hungry, he still doubted he could have swum through those breakers and lived.

Nonetheless he disengaged the thwart and started paddling. The slowness of his approach to shore would have maddened a human. Theor was chiefly conscious of the pain in his flesh and the burning in his gills. Time was lost in a fever dream. When at last the cliffs opened and a narrow fjord was revealed, he took a while to realise what it meant.

But — 'Ulloala, the Powers are favourable yet!' He threw his remaining energy into frantic labour. The ammonia flew behind each stroke, the wreckage moved sluggishly forward, the calm-looking bay waxed before him.

And ceased to do so. He was making no further progress. When his muscles gave out and he had to sink back onto the struts to rest, he saw the fjord recede. He couldn't enter.

He risked raising himself high for a better look. Waves licked around a comparatively flat region that fanned out of the fjord's mouth for a mile or more, until it mingled with the general unrest. At the inner end of the bay he glimpsed a grey sheen, coming down the slopes and into the ammonia.

His quasi-boat lurched and nearly capsized. Hastily he crouched back down and considered the situation. His skull seemed full of sand, but inch by inch he ploughed his way to an explanation.

The Jovian surface rarely gets so cold that ammonia freezes, but it can happen when a highland is exposed to air masses pushing down from the poles. Such a glacier flows more quickly, under the prevailing gravitational field, than its terrestrial analogue. When it reaches the sea, it does not form icebergs, for the solid phase of ammonia is denser than the liquid. Big chunks break off and sink to the bottom. But when the depth is not great, they melt rather rapidly. A torrent was pouring from the fjord. Perhaps a sidewheel ship could have bucked it, but Theor could not.

Ush, he thought, *I'll just have to hope the next inlet is friendlier.*

But he could not fool himself long. He had seen the maps drawn by navigators who ventured north. Crude though they were, they had enough information to write an end to such hopes. The current would soon sweep him into The

Kettles, where it met a long headland surrounded by reefs and broke into turbulence that would kill him quite as dead as the surf yonder. He might as well try a landing here.

'Mark,' he called. Only the sea answered, and he remembered that Fraser was gone. Hurgh ... no matter ... it was fatuous to expect the Earthman had any further counsel.

Or – wait. Wait a sliver of time. Had Fraser not told once, infinitely long ago ... ? Theor fumbled through the darkness in his head. There was a memory ... moving pictures shown in the House of the Oracles – *Surfboarding*, he'd named it. If you had a plank, and caught the very lip of a breaker, it would carry you unbroken to land.

And ... the outrigger was flat-topped, with a false keel. It was large enough to bear his weight alone.

Strength sprang from some final interior source. Theor began to paddle again.

When he was near, could feel the first shivers of swell and hear nothing but the wrath under the cliffs, he drew his knife and got to work. It was slow and toilsome, treading ammonia and clinging with one hand while the other sawed away at the lashings which held the struts. He had lost impatience, though, lost both hope and fear. For him there was only a succession of tasks; he did not even recall their ultimate purpose.

In the end, the outrigger floated free. He scrambled on top, thrice turning turtle before he managed the trick. Belly down, legs wrapped around the board, he dug in his paddle.

A wave took him. He felt how he climbed and gathered speed. Foam blew past, momentarily blinding. He remembered that he must get to the crest and stay there, or be crushed. Furiously, he thrust away. His clumsy craft added its little speed to the waves, and he got where he had to be. He rose to a crouched stance and the surf bore him landward.

There fell a weird quietness, only a hiss around his head

and an underground rumble that shuddered in his guts. From his height, which grew ever greater, he looked down the curving cliff that was the front of the wave, and saw with abnormal clarity how foam-streaked and intricately wrinkled it was. The trough lay nearly black beneath him. and the shore came close with dizzying speed. He had dropped his paddle – no matter, useless now, all he could do was maintain position by shifting his weight from front to back, side to side. Probably no untrained human could have lived through that rush. But Theor had nonhuman senses, and came from a line who for many generations had dealt with natural forces. He rode the wave in.

It peaked and broke. He flew through the air, struck with a crash that would have knocked the wind out of anyone who depended on lungs, and fought his way back to the surface. The sea boiled around him. Tossed like a chip, he had a final sense of saying farewell to existence. *So let the thunder have me.* His feet brushed bottom. The undertow yanked them from beneath him. He stopped swimming, sank, clawed himself fast to the sand, and slugged his way ahead.

The shallows ... a staggering run ... dry beach, and collapse, and night spinning down over him.

When he awoke, the sun had gone below the western fog banks. The surf bellowed and tumbled in the last dun light. The cliffs rose gigantic from the detritus slope on which he lay. He thought he saw a possible route for climbing them. But beyond there could only be wilderness. And he was alone, with a single knife for a weapon.

11

Fraser sat for a while staring at the transceiver, until he clenched both fists and brought them down on the panel. The blow rang through silence and shadows. A beam of sunlight pierced the forward viewport making veins and knobbly knuckles stand forth with a certain cruelty. Noticing that reminded him how he still ached from over-exertion. *Nuts! forty isn't old. But it can sure feel that way. Oh stop snivelling. Make yourself presentable. You smell like a dead billy goat.*

Stiffly, he got up and moved to the rear of the gannycat. Danny Mendoza had turned it over to him when he said he had to contact Jupiter, so he could use its communication equipment and have room to stretch out between calls. He stripped, drew some water into a basin, and sponged his skin. There wasn't much sense in cleaning up, just to meet a she-quisling – well, morale – and she *was* attractive in her fashion. He grinned lopsidedly at himself.

Memory ran back to the hour when she had slipped him the note. That had been in Aurora rather than Swayne's battleship headquarters – doubtless to make sure no one came to the conference after a hearty meal of dynamite, and lit a cigar. Fraser had accompanied Sam Hoshi. Lorraine was there too, and a couple of senior Navy officers. Supposedly she represented the town. Everyone sat on the edge of their chairs, in the bleak, crowded room: except Swayne, behind the desk, who overpowered the scene. Not that he shouted, or even scolded; but he had the self-possession of victory.

His hands sliced the air. 'Let's stop exchanging swear words,' he said. 'From my viewpoint, you are insurrectionists. You killed and wounded a number of loyal men. Your casualties are less than you deserve.'

Hoshi opened his mouth, snapped it shut again, and writhed his fingers together. Two of his sons lay dead outside.

Swayne quirked a smile that went no further than his eyes. 'You, of course, look at it differently,' he continued. 'Nobody's opinion is likely to be changed here and now. Well, I am a professional fighter. I'm willing to admit you're sincere, however misguided. The problem is not one of emotional attitudes, but of what to do. I'm more interested in getting on with the job than in immediate justice.'

'What about justice later on, though, when the political cops arrive?' Fraser demanded. 'Why should we give in, if we're to be arrested inside a year, jailed, shot, or brainwashed?'

Lorraine's thick fair brows drew into a frown. 'That last is a nasty word, Mark,' she said.

'So call it re-education,' he answered. 'I'd still rather die on my feet.'

'I can't give you any absolute guarantees,' Swayne confessed. 'However, think a bit. The restored government will have its hands full on Earth and the inner planets for a long time to come. Why should it waste effort on a bunch of isolated colonists, especially if I put in a good word for you? Cooperate with me, and you have my promise as an officer of the United States Space Force that I will.'

Fraser saw the taut face and believed. As for the police and the courts — yes, there was a pretty fair chance that Swayne had also called that turn correctly. Nonetheless, defeat was a jagged lump to swallow.

Hoshi leaned forward. 'There are five thousand people in the Jovian System,' he said tonelessly. 'A lot fewer than a single one of your missiles would kill on Earth. Not to mention everybody who'd go before a firing squad, back there if not here. On balance, we ought to let the whole colony die if that can stop you.'

'It can't though,' Swayne said. 'It would be a setback, yes, but the *Vega* would still be at large. There are other places we might go, certain asteroids, for instance. Not as suitable as this, but worth trying if Ganymede is knocked out. I don't believe you're able to accomplish that, anyway.'

He leaned forward, bridging his fingers, nailing the visitors with his eyes. 'Admit the facts,' he said. 'You're beaten. The only duty you have left is to your wives and children. I repeat my offer: withdraw to your homes, and make no further trouble, and we'll leave you alone in turn,'

'You can even take along those people who want to leave Aurora,' Lorraine added. 'And the rest of us will continue the flow of essential supplies to you.'

'Nice gimmick,' Hoshi snorted. 'Get rid of potential mutineers and saboteurs, huh?'

'Of course,' said Swayne. 'But are you so inhuman that you won't take them in?'

He talks of inhumanity! Fraser thought. *I'll never understand Homo Sapiens.*

Maybe that's why I like Theor so much. Anxiety touched him. *I should get back to the vehicle. He may have called.*

The talk dragged on, endlessly, meaninglessly. 'We can't pull out at once,' Hoshi said. 'We've wounded to care for.'

'I'll send out the hospital staff,' Lorraine promised.

'I want you out of here fast,' Swayne insisted; and the haggling began anew.

In the end, the mean little bargain was struck. The Ganymedeans rose. 'Good day to you,' Swayne dismissed them, and began studying some papers.

Lorraine went over to Fraser. He was already at the door, sick to get away. 'Mark,' she said.

He gave her his coldest stare.

'Mark, I'm so sorry.'

'You ought to be.' He opened the door.

'Can't you understand? I have to do what's right, the same as you. And how can we know what's right? It isn't something you weigh or measure. No –' She looked away. Her teeth caught her lower lip. 'It can tear you apart.'

She had put on a dress for this occasion, severe in cut but still revealing of long legs and high bosom. Tears blurred the emerald eyes. He remembered shared work and shared laughter, and could not hate her.

'Would you shake hands?' she whispered.

Hoshi wasn't looking. Fraser's arm jerked forward. She caught his hand in a spasmodic motion. Her other hand closed over the clasp, bending his fingers. He felt a small stiff object. She shook her head, ever so faintly. His heart banged. He slipped it into his pocket, feeling as if the entire cosmos watched.

'So long, Mark,' Lorraine said. She turned and walked from him, out the opposite door.

He followed Hoshi to the nearest airlock. A pair of armed spacemen tramped behind. The corridors were deserted. Most of Aurora's population had been ordered behind doors while the emergency lasted. Hoshi moved slumpshouldered, speaking not a word. Fraser's head was in too much of a whirl to attempt any remark.

Besides, what could the conquered say?

Alone again in Mendoza's cat, he took out the card. She had scrawled on it: *Meet me behind the moonships at 0800 next cycle. Don't let anyone know.*

Ganymede's day equalled 7.15 of Earth's. The colonists measured time in twenty-four-hour units, Alpha Cycle, Bravo Cycle, and on through Gable, with Harry a truncated addendum. There were too few people on the other moons to make a different system worthwhile for them. The rendezvous was upon him.

But what the devil did she want? To explain herself

97

further? To offer me – He dismissed that possibility with a wary chuckle. Face the fact, he was an ugly old married man. Not that occasional thoughts hadn't crossed his mind ... And this was no damned time for them, while Eve waited beyond the mountains, and Sam Hoshi prepared for the homeward retreat, and Sam's boys were blocks of ice on the lava, along with Pat Mahoney and so many others.

Fraser completed his bath, squeezed the sponge into the basin and emptied that into the reclaimer, ran a depilator over his bristly features and a comb through his hair. Long John, spacesuit, pass through the lock and look around. The colonial fleet glimmered in ranks under the brutal mass of Apache Crater. Men moved about here and there on various errands, in and out of shadows cast by the westering sun. But they were few; most sagged in their vehicles, waiting only to depart. Stars crowded the eastern horizon above the Glenn peaks, and Jupiter swelled enormously toward half phase at the zenith. Nonetheless, darkness dominated the land.

Fraser kept to the gloom until he was behind the crater, then cut due east to put Aurora out of sight. Landmarks were like old friends, showing him how to circle around and approach the field again from the north, unseen. But he had an irrational feeling that they had stiffened into the same voicelessness as his dead.

The clustered vessels rose before him. A figure stepped out from among them, took his arm, and led him back to their shelter. Helmet rang against helmet in a cave of night.

'Oh, Mark!' Both her hands clutched at him. 'I didn't know if you'd trust me enough to come. Thank you, thank you.'

He shifted awkwardly from foot to foot. 'Why, uh, shouldn't I?'

'It could have been a trick. Remember, your escape was the first successful defiance. He was furious, in that cold creepy way of his, he talked about making an example of you. I didn't know if he might not seize you when you came yestercycle, in spite of everything. And yet, when we arranged for the conference, I had to suggest your name, had to ask you to come along, not being sure, not knowing if he'd respect your immunity or – kill you.' The words tumbled from her, broken by unsteady breaths. 'I told him you were, you are one of the most important men in the colony, you could better speak for your side than anyone else, even Hoshi.'

'That's not so. I, uh, you know I never was any kind of politician or leader. Not forceful enough, don't have enough sense of human relations. I almost refused.'

'I never feared that. You have too much sense of duty.'

'Huh? No, ridiculous. And to hell with it, anyhow. So you risked my life to arrange this meeting. Why?'

'I risked my own too,' she said defensively.

'You?' he jeered. 'The white-haired girl of the glorious counterrevolution?'

'Mark, I'm on your side!'

He could only gape into lightlessness.

'I didn't approve of the Sam Halls,' said the hurried, muffled voice. 'I thought they were honest but mistaken. Maybe I still do, I don't know, everything is so confused. But I *can't* go along with a man who ... who'd do something like that ... turn nuclear weapons on his own country. On any country that hasn't done it first! I sat alone and cried, oh, God, I was scared and sick –'

'But you've collaborated,' he said stupidly.

'Yes. Don't you see? The call went out over the intercom. For volunteers. I had to do something. What else could I do, but get myself into a position where maybe, somehow, I could sabotage – They'd already inquired about a lot of us. They don't have psychoprobe equipment, or I'd never have fooled them. But they do have a couple of tough political officers who know how to, to interrogate. They knew that everyone thought I must be on their side. So when I volunteered – Not that they took me on faith. I still see those two men in my dreams, barking question after question after question. But I got through it. Don't ask me how, but I did. Now I'm mayor. I keep the city running, and act as a go-between. They, the people, they obey, but I know how most of them loathe me. I can almost hear them thinking: *If we can only get rid of the ship, that bitch'll wish she never was born, even more than I do now!'*

She gulped and was still.

'I beg your humble pardon, Lory,' Fraser said.

When she didn't answer, he asked: 'What's the situation like in there?'

'Queer,' she said in a wondering tone. 'I'd never imagined how queer it would be. You think of occupation as being like everybody in jail. But no, life goes on, in a crippled fashion. People still have jobs to do. They still go home at the end of a watch, and cook dinner, and play cards or talk or ... whatever. Only a few vital points are guarded. And the guards, well, they aren't exactly jailers. People have occasion to talk with them, and one word leads to another. You know, here's this boy from Iowa so you ask him if he knows your cousin Joe and how the new Des Moines rocketport looks. Or looked. Maybe the fighting wrecked it; neither you nor he know ... Some men, who made open trouble, are under arrest, but they aren't mistreated and you can visit them at certain hours. Even the out-and-out collaborators have their human side. They're still the folks you used to work with, chat with, invite to parties. You look for a change in them and can't see any. Only there's this wall around them, it's invisible and sound passes through, but something is strained out –' She gave a forlorn laugh. 'I'm talking as if I were an ordinary colonist. Actually, of course, I'm a collaborator myself.'

'Are any of the others faking it like you?' Fraser inquired.

'I don't know. I haven't dared approach them. Maybe they don't dare approach me. Still, I doubt it. Nearly all you settlers have been away from Earth so long that you've got politically naïve. You aren't used to, well, handling official jargon while thinking of something else. I believe most of you, trying to be sleepers, would soon make some word or gesture that didn't ring true. And at once you'd be under suspicion and off to the brig with you.'

'What's a sleeper?'

'See, that's what I mean. You don't know as much as any child does at home. A sleeper is one like me. No, I think the other collaborators are genuine, some out of sincerity, some out of fear or opportunism. Of course, if we could destroy Swayne, they'd all claim to have been Sam Hall fifth columnists!'

Like you, Lory? Fraser forced the question away with an effort. 'How many are there?'

'A couple of hundred. And fewer spacemen than that, of whom some have to stand watch aboard the *Vega*. It's the real threat. Without it – I won't call that thing "she"! – we could overpower the crew in no time, even if they do have the only firearms. But as long as it can shell the city . . . well, the loyal people bide their time, hoping something will turn up. Which makes them collaborators of a sort too, doesn't it?'

'Also us, Hoshi's men, after today,' Fraser sighed. 'How's the warhead manufacture coming along?'

'We're still getting organised. I have to say "we" – part of my work is personnel screening. Mostly production can be automated, but a few engineers and technies will be needed to set up the plant, and a few more to run it, plus others to mine the ores, bring them in, refine them and deliver the isotopes. Every colonial will be under guard every minute he works, naturally; but even so, we have to assemble a pre-

101

dictable staff, shall I say. Not necessarily devoted to the cause, but obedient. We can do it, too, by evaluating the psych records in the medical files. That takes time, though, and of course I'm as inefficient as I dare be.'

'I wonder ... it occurs to me ... is every man in the ship's crew reliable?'

'Yes. Career military personnel always got thorough probing at intervals, you know, especially in a sensitive organisation like the Space Force. Swayne told me he'd only had to send three men out the airlock. Only!'

'Well – ' Fraser searched for words. Silence pressed in so heavily that he didn't stop to polish them. 'Okay. What do you want with me?'

'You're the one man I can trust who might possibly be able to help,' she told him.

'Huh? How?'

'You're a good space pilot.'

'You mean you can smuggle me onto a moonship? That's useless.'

'More useless than you realise. Every one of these boats has had the air bed off and the reaction regulator taken out. It'll only be put back in when an absolutely essential trip has to be made; and then a couple of guards will go along. There are no free ships left on the other moons, either. Before your army arrived, Swayne sent his boats out. The Traffic Control records told them where to look. They shot a small missile at each parked ship. Partly that's a precaution against someone trying a suicide dive onto the *Vega* – though its guns could doubtless abort any such attempt quite easily. Mainly, though, it's to tighten his hold on us. If we don't behave, our people on Io and Callisto and the other moons will be left to starve. Or maybe gunned down – there's a picket boat in orbit around each one.'

'I see.' Fraser swallowed. His palms felt clammy. 'What do you have in mind?'

'He overlooked one ship. And she's got the acceleration to reach Earth in time to warn them.'

'Come again?'

'The *Olympia*.'

'But –'

'I know. Her mission was postponed because of the trouble on Jupiter, and she's not yet stocked with food, water, or anything else for life support. But she's otherwise set to go!'

'And with so much else on their minds – and the ship sitting right under the *Vega*'s guns – yes.' The blood pounded in Fraser's ears and at the base of his throat. 'If the stuff could, somehow, be smuggled aboard –'

'I don't know how. I haven't had much time to think myself. But maybe we can figure out a way. And you can drive her, can't you?'

'How'd I ever get aboard? Hoshi's leaving before sundown.'

'Come into the city with me. Entry is safe, especially in the confusion there'll be when the evacuees go out. Not too many of them, actually; essential personnel won't be allowed to go; but still, quite a number. You can hide in my place and we'll make plans when I'm off duty. We may lose a little weight, sharing one ration between us, but *I* don't mind. The risk is pretty horrible, I know. I won't blame you in the least for refusing. You've got a family, I don't, it makes a difference. But this is just all I can think of to do.'

To be free again.

No, that was a phrase for a 3V melodrama. Fraser looked at the implication and his bowels cramped inside him. Captain Manly Valiant, Terror of the Spaceways, might load a few tons of necessities on a wheelbarrow, ram it through a cordon of guards, vault into the ship and be on his way before the astonished villains had gotten the wax out of their moustaches. But Mark Fraser, now, had seen an

103

army macerated, a man die in his arms, a leader bend the neck and go home with two cold lumps which had once been dear to him. Mark Fraser had Eve, Ann, and Colin to look after. He had endured arbitrary government in the past, grumblingly, but not finding life too bad; he knew perfectly well that he could endure it again if he must. He was aging and staid and had learned that man's fate is a series of compromises. He saw no way to accomplish anything but his own heroic death, and doubted that there would be much heroism. He would scream as loudly as the next slob when a laser beam punctured his belly; or cringe from their boots when they caught him. . . .

Foulest thought of all: this woman admitted that Swayne wanted his head. While Fraser was with Hoshi's men, he came under the general amnesty. But if he was lured into the city and arrested, Ganymede wouldn't revolt again merely to save him. In fact, his execution would be one more blow at the spirit of his fellows: maybe the last one that was needed before they made the interior surrender.

'What do you want to do, Mark?'

He barely heard through the querning in his brain.

'Anything you decide is right by me,' she told him. 'But you have to decide now.'

'I hope – ' His voice betrayed him with a squeak. He tried again. 'I hope you've got some happypills in your place, Lory.'

12

Theoretically, the most efficient procedure would have been to sleep in dormitories, eat in messhalls, and share a few washrooms. In practice, privacy was an urgent need. Every apartment had complete facilities, and Aurorans were not in the habit of dropping in on each other unannounced. Moreover, Lorraine was under a social boycott by the majority. Fraser had little fear of being surprised.

Nonetheless his nervousness grew. Bachelor quarters amounted to a bed-sitting room, plus a tiny kitchen and bath. He felt trapped. And there was no tobacco, and his belly growled for more food than was available, and the small supply of psych medicine had to be saved for times of real need. The first 'night' they were together, he and the woman had talked in circles, finding no answer, until sheer exhaustion put them to sleep; and, while a floor didn't make too stiff a bed in this gravity, he had slept ill.

She went back to work after breakfast, and he settled down to business. Whatever scheme they arrived at must be mostly his. Her mind was too occupied with maintaining her balance on the tightrope. For several hours his thoughts kept straying beyond the Glenns. Hoshi would have returned by now, bearing that letter he had scribbled for Eve.

The leader had protested, called Fraser a lunatic, insisted that at least a younger man go with Lorraine. 'No, I'm afraid not,' Fraser had said. 'You see, the guys who were supposed to pilot the *Olympia,* who're briefed and trained, they're inaccessible. One's in the brig for assaulting a Navy man, and the other, well, she isn't sure about him. We can't multiply risks more than we have to, can we? And in the getaway, the ship may have to dive into Jupiter's atmosphere to escape pursuit. That's not a situation an ordinary rocket jockey can handle. But I've piloted submersibles, back on Earth. The *Olympia* design is based on terrestrial bathyscaphes.' He shrugged. A tic in his cheek continued the gesture. 'I wish to hell I could find a substitute. But if the job's to have any chance of success, I seem to be elected.'

In the end, Hoshi regarded him for minutes before saying, 'Okay. And . . . win or lose, I envy your son.'

Would Eve understand as much?

She seemed very remote, the recollection of her blurred by his immediacies, as if she were someone he had known in a past that had long slipped through his fingers. Reality was these walls, the start in his pulse when feet passed in the corridor outside, the absence of his pipe, the occasional wondering whether Theor had gotten safely to land, the dreary round of plans for stocking the escape vessel and perception of their flimsiness.

Item: Several guards were always posted on the field around the *Vega*. They'd see anyone who carried stores aboard the *Olympia,* and questions would follow.

Item: Spacesuits had been returned to their owners after the colonial army left. One of Lorraine's man-sized spares – every locker held extras – would equip Fraser for the sprint from a city airlock to the ship. But he'd never make the distance before a sentry shot him.

Item: Lorraine might conceivably get together a few men who were willing to die in an attack on the guards, while Fraser used the diversion to get away. But sounding them out, overcoming their suspicions of her, assembling their gear, would take many cycles. In that long a time, Swayne might very well disable the *Olympia;* some collaborationist could remind him of her potential. Besides, Lorraine wasn't blindly trusted. She was hardly ever alone outside her dwelling – the nature of her work made that inevitable – and an eye was kept upon her. If she started having a number of visitors here, that would soon be noticed and investigated. In any event, the supply problem wouldn't be solved thus.

I got too damn fired up. I should have thought of this before committing myself. That ship might as well be in orbit around Alpha Centauri.

No, wait. What do you do when a problem looks insoluble? You back up and look at it from another angle. A different approach.

I'm too tense. Okay, I'll invest one of those pills in the project.

He swallowed coolness and determination, sprawled on the bed and turned his analytical mind loose. The answer grew before him.

Lorraine came in. She shut the door behind her as Fraser sat up. 'Hello,' she said. 'How're you doing?'

Her voice was dull and there were shadows under her eyes. Yet she moved elastically, and he noticed her high colour and thought how much more she had in the way of looks than any conventional prettiness.

'I may have our answer,' he said.

'You do?' Weariness vanished from her like fog burned off the sea by a morning sun. She reached the bed in a jump and clasped his shoulders. 'I knew you could!'

'Whoa, there. Let's talk this over and see what the holes in the scheme are.' Still, he felt a glow, and if it was mostly chemical, was it any the less real for that?

'Sure. But you wouldn't say you "may" have licked something unless you knew you had.' She pirouetted across the room. 'Whee!'

'Good Lord, Lory, you're acting like – ' for some reason he stopped before saying 'my daughter' – 'like a kid let out of school.'

'That's how I feel, too. With an end in sight to this horror, why not? Look, I've got a bottle of whisky I've been saving for some extra-special occasion. What say we break it out now?'

'I don't like the taste of alcohol. Often wish I did, but I guess we all have some handicap or other. Don't let me stop you, of course. Only, well, we do have to discuss this seriously.'

'Uh-huh.' She sobered, though the vibrancy remained in her tone. 'I'll start dinner, with something nice that I've been saving too, and while it cooks we can be earnest.' She flushed a bit. 'I'd like to change clothes, also.'

'Sure.' He retreated to the bathroom till she said he could come back. A close-fitting black dress with a single aluminum-bronze pin, a stylised comet, did her a disturbing amount of justice. Light gleamed in her hair's gold. He sat down and tried to arrange his thoughts while she bustled in the kitchen.

Returning, she took a chair opposite his. 'All right, Mark,' she said. 'What's your proposal?'

'Well –' He squirmed about and stared past her, at a picture on the wall. It wasn't the sentimental Earth land-scape of the average colonial home; NGC 5457 coiled stark and glittering in space. 'Well, the problem breaks into two parts; provisioning the ship and getting aboard her. Then a little warmup time is needed, and time to accelerate before a gun or a missile can hit, but that's part of the whole boarding operation. What hung us up was assuming the two phases had to be in that order.'

She slapped her knee. 'I think I get your idea. Why *didn't* I see? But go on.'

'There are still radiophone lines to every outlying settle-ment, and with so much else to do, I don't imagine Swayne's gang monitors them.'

'N-no. I have to make fairly frequent calls outside of

town, to the mines for instance, and I can choose a moment when I'm alone in my office. Who should I contact?'

'The people at Blocksberg. It's nearly antipodal to Aurora, you recall, and Gebhardt was with us, so I'm certain they'll cooperate. He can check your bona fides with Sam Hoshi if he wants. It'd be better to alert somebody on one of the other moons, but that goes through a different circuit –'

'Which isn't automatic, and the operators are collaborationists. Besides, you couldn't get undetected past the picket boats. They're posted on radar watch against ships from Earth, mainly, but each one has some missiles. Okay, Blocksberg. I tell them to have your supplies ready for quick loading, right?'

'Yes. The boxes can be slung through the cargo hatch in five minutes, and I can restow them when I'm in space. I won't need too much. The crossing won't take a dreadful lot of days. Mainly I'll need air, water, food and interplanetary navigation equipment, including an ephemeris and reduction tables. Nobody can cross the Solar System by the seat of his pants! Drugs would be helpful. With Antion I can pass nearer the sun than the screens would otherwise permit, and so shorten the passage time. And I'd prefer not to spend a week in hospital on Earth, recovering from the effects of so much high and zero gee, so booster pills would also be nice. But I can get along without the medicine chest if I have to.'

'Check. You'll blast off from here, then, and hop to Blocksberg?'

'Yes. On a long curve, maybe clear around Jupiter, so their radar won't tell them where I'm bound. In fact, I'll start out in such a way that it'll seem I'm headed for another moon. I can reach any Galilean satellite without instruments or data, given as much reaction mass to waste as I know the *Olympia* has.'

'But are you sure that what's-his-name, Gebhardt, has

the equipment you want?'

'I'm sure he does not. Why should he? But the Glory Hole isn't far from his place, and you remember it has a small, unmanned emergency spacefield. He can raid the depot there. I don't dare land directly at the field, because Swayne might expect that.'

'You'll have to allow a few cycles for them to assemble your stuff.'

'I know. Now as for Phase One of the plan, that depends on you. You've got to sneak me out of town.'

'Hm. I've worried about that. They've gotten awfully cautious. Most of the airlocks are sealed off, and there's a guard at every one still operational. You can't take a cat without a crewman accompanying you.'

'I don't want one. I only have to get out on foot, with some tools.'

'Still not easy. They require a pass. But tell me what you have in mind.'

'I'll walk beyond the horizon, circle around, and get in among the moonships. They won't see me if I come from the north, as I did in meeting you. You told me the reaction regulators have been sequestered. Well, I'll go aboard one of the boats, dismantle the safety cutoffs, and start the engine.'

'What? It'll blow up!'

'Not exactly. Not like a bomb, anyhow. But there'll be some fancy fireworks. If that doesn't give me a chance to sneak into the *Olympia,* I resign.'

Lorraine stared at her feet. 'You could get killed, Mark,' she said.

'There'll be time to get clear before the engine blows. The warmup period is much less than for a thing the size of the *Vega,* but it still amounts to several minutes. The surrounding ships will screen off radiation pretty well. As for the *Olympia*'s own warmup, I count on things being so confused that nobody will notice she's purring.'

'Well – Damn! I don't like it.'

'You have a better idea?'

'I haven't any,' she said in a thin voice.

He leaned over and patted her hand. 'Don't be such a worrywart, kid. I've even calculated my schedule. Ninety seconds from the moonship cluster to the *Olympia*. Thirty seconds to open the cargo hatch and get inside.'

'Longer than that. The accommodation ladder isn't there. You'd have to scramble up the jacks and balance yourself somehow, holding on with one hand while you undog the hatch with the other.'

'Well – '

'Two people could manage a lot faster,' she said. 'One standing on the other's shoulders, see? Also, there's the problem of getting you out. I tell you, you can't simply wander up to one of those sentries and ask him to let you through. I could try to fake a pass for you, but it'd be risky as the devil.'

In spite of her words, she was looking happier. 'What do you propose?' he asked.

'That I go along.'

'You're crazy!'

'No. Look. I can manufacture an excuse to go out, myself, with no trouble. I'll tell the entry control officer that I've gotten word of equipment failure at the Navajo diggings, and it might be sabotage. So I'll tell him I want to stroll over, make an inspection, and fix it myself. I've been doing a little electronics repair work right along, we're so shorthanded. I'll have him write a pass for me and an assistant, like say Chris Coulter; only I'll have seen to it that Chris is working on the other side of town that watch. The sentry knows what I look like, everybody does by now, but he'll hardly know one technie in Aurora from another. He'll let us through, *and* a bag of tools. I'll help you detonate the moonship, board the *Olympia* with you, and get off at Blocksberg.'

'But – reprisals against you – '

'Gosh, I'll be safer out of town than in, once this thing breaks. Though I don't imagine Swayne will do much when he sees you're well away. He can't fight nuclear-armed ships that have been warned about him. He may surrender; or he may pull out; or at worst, he may hold Aurora hostage and bargain for a pardon. But he'll know he's lost the war.'

'Even so ... well, yes, I'll be glad to have you clear of him. Agreed!'

She thrust out her hand. Her eyes held a Valkyrie light. Their clasps joined, and they looked long at each other.

Suddenly he kissed her. She hung back an instant, then responded, and it lasted quite a while.

Breaking away, with a shaky laugh, she said: 'I'd better go tend our celebration dinner.'

'I suppose,' he mumbled.

'Would ... would you ... are you sure you won't have a drink?'

'No. But go ahead yourself.'

'I will. I need one.'

They talked until very late, and she told him more of her past then was entirely wise, and he had a great deal of trouble getting to sleep afterward, down on the floor.

13

Westward and upward. Somewhere beyond these coastal heights, there was a range which Nyarrans called the Furious Mountains, and then the wild highlands of Rollarik where perhaps Walfilo's army still wandered. But surely they were unreachable.

Theor climbed on. There was nothing else to do, except yield to his weariness and die. The wind harried about him, thin and cold, piping among crags and throwing streamers of ruddy mist into his eyes. That fog closed off vision after a few yards; he crept over dark, wetly gleaming ice-rocks in absolute solitude. Somewhere to his right sounded the rush of a stream. He wondered if he should seek it out and try to catch a fish as he had done further down, his last food in a longer time than he could readily recall. But no, the danger of losing his footing in the canyon was too great in proportion to the slight chance of success. A fall is a more serious matter on Jupiter than on Earth, even for a Jovian. As for the likelihood of making a catch, once he put the shoreline forest behind him he had entered a land that seemed altogether barren.

He could guess why. The dry fire in his gills cut through a lightheadedness that made his universe half unreal. Under the gravity of this planet, the change of air pressure with altitude is several times as great as in the terrestrial case. He was not much more than a mile above sea level, but less than half the concentration of hydrogen for which his body was designed now circulated through the intricate spiracles. Ever oftener must he stop to rest, kneebones locked, head

113

drooping, hearts a-hammer as if to burst, while fragments of dream jeered at him.

Mountains so tall are rare on Jupiter. Though unthinkable energies are locked in the highly compressed core and mantle, and burst out as earthquake, volcano, geyser, or that upwelling into the atmosphere which creates the thirty-thousand-mile-long permanent storm men call the Red Spot – still, erosion and gravity offer savage opposition to orogenic processes. There is not enough strongly elevated ground at any given time for land life to adapt to it.

The backbone of this range could not be far off. Nothing else was physically possible. Staggering, stumbling, clawing his way with all six limbs past ridges and over talus slopes that rattled beneath his feet, Theor wondered in a dull way whether anyone would ever bestride the passes. Surely not he, enfeebled by hunger and alone. But he had to keep trying: for the Ulunt-Khazul ringed in the city where Leenant and Pors were.

He looked ahead, as if he might see an end. But only the tumbled mineral waste lay before him, soon hidden in the mist. Ammonia vapour blown off the sea and condensing to pour back in numberless rivers and rivulets, those clouds had hues abnormal to him, brown, onsy, stawr, piled in heavy banks against precipice and gorge wall; and his feelers drank strange sharp taste-odours.

The light here was equally weird. Despite the overcast, it was about as much as on a good day in Nyarr, for less absorbing atmosphere lay above. But Theor was used to a certain distribution of infrared wavelengths. These cold stones sheened otherwise than the warmer plain of Medalon.

For the hundredth time, he thumbed the switch on his communicator locket. Only the wind answered his call. Not that it would have made any difference, he thought. What could Fraser do for him now? But the voice of a friend would have been comforting.

Ah, well. He braced himself and continued. Because of the low angle of repose on Jupiter, his traverse had involved little climbing in the sense that a terrestrial mountaineer would have understood. Otherwise he would never have gotten this far. *I am near the end of what I can do, though,* he realized. And a part of him was glad to think about a final rest.

Another part kept his legs in motion.

The fog thickened. He remembered how he drifted after the storm, oh, many cosmic cycles ago. But this was a closing in such as he had never experienced. He walked through deeply coloured smokes, where the wind was muffled but curious shrill trillings sounded from time to time. What air there was became acrid in his gills. Yet these weren't volcano fumes, he thought dimly. What, then? The Hidden Folk were said to lair hereabouts, north of Jonnary, and brew magic . . .

He had seen a number of the flakes before he noticed them.

Another swarm blew by. He reached out and caught one. It squirmed in his hand. He brought it close to his eyes, to see in the thickening murk. The shape was a lacy little eight-pointed star. Hundreds had been in each of the flocks. He touched his antennae to the surface. Peculiar essence, but – With an animal impulse, he popped it into his mouth and crunched. The bit of flesh was oily and quite foreign in taste. It went down, though, and his stomach accepted it.

It went down!

Theor stood bewildered. He was too worn to feel any great emotion. Chiefly he was conscious of puzzlement. There couldn't be anything alive up here. Only there was. He had just eaten it.

Wait. His mind creaked toward the obvious. *Food, if I can catch enough. But how?*

At home I could make a bag from a darva leaf. The common, primitive plant grew in broad sheets that lay flat on the ground. *Nothing like that here.* Thinking was so difficult that he went over to the formal language. *Negation of former statement. Where one biological type can exist, variant structures will indubitably also occur, utilising the first sort as well as each other. For life is forever a wholeness, and it has faded my spirit to be the only animate thing in this realm. My best course of action is to seek further. There appears to be some elevated life zone, whose lower fringe I have penetrated.* Again he heard a high, liquid piping. Though echoes and fog confused sound, he thought it came from above. *Accordingly, I am behoven to proceed.*

Thin though it was, the chance put heart back in him. He trudged on with something akin to eagerness.

So dense did the clouds get, and so intently was he looking and listening for overhead traces, that he almost went over a cliff edge. Barely in time, he stopped, and stood for a while trembling.

The mountainside was chopped off as if by an axe. Impassably steep and slick, it dropped away into the tinted vapour drifts. The surface shimmered with condensation. Theor found a loose rock and tossed it over the verge. He heard it strike and go skittering, down and down and down, until the noise died, and still no bottom had been struck. Sick with dismay, he recognised that this was probably the topmost point of his route, but also probably the end. The musical calls, out beyond sight, mocked at him.

Ush, he scolded himself, *I may as well perish moving.* Because the declivity curved slightly eastward on his right, he scrambled in that direction. He was careful not to look over the brink again.

The wind flowed behind him, around him, driving the wet coils before it. Another flight of star-shapes blew past, not within arm's length.

A whistle sounded. He glanced back, jumped around with a curse, and crouched against a spur. His knife rasped out of the sheath. But he was ignored. Vast and vague in the fog, the thing passed by above the gorge. A man would have likened it to a whale, with long fins and a nest of fine tendrils around the mouth. Those were gathering in the tiny living flakes, and the creature swam on into nothingness. Theor did not follow for several minutes.

A life zone indeed, he thought shakenly. *Airborne, inhabiting these upper regions – and we never knew. But we belong to the dark depths.*

He recalled Fraser telling him that spectroscopy indicated that Jupiter had a dense microbial population in the high atmosphere. The discovery had not seemed important to Theor. What was the significance, if organisms too small to see floated above the clouds? But if they supported larger species, which supported larger ones yet . . . why, his whole world was inside a shell of life!

Had his wits been less blunted, he could have reasoned on the basis of physics and chemistry he had learned from the humans. At his present height, and well beyond, the Jovian air is still dense enough to upbear objects of considerable specific gravity. And minerals are suspended in the clouds: notably sodium, whose complexes with ammonia help make the planet a colourful sight from space, but also much else – micrometeoritic infall of iron, silicon, magnesium, phosphorus, and oxides. Getting more energy from above than the surface does, these atmospheric layer¬ are correspondingly more able to support hydrogen-ammonia photosynthesis.

In fact, it seems probable that Jovian life originated at great altitudes, and that it remains more abundant there than on land and sea. Though the planetwide ecology has yet to be worked out, one may theorise that the surface population is dependent on what drifts down from above – not to the same extent as life on Earth's ocean bed, for plants do exist, but nonetheless critically so.

Theor could only think of plans, each more hopeless than the last, for trapping something to eat.

He continued on his way for a while. A dim mass grew out of the vapours. When he saw what it was, he stood long alone with the thought that here might be the ultimate goal of his journey. A wall rose before him, straight across his path, from the cliff on his left to the unseen on his right.

I could try to go around, or retrace my steps and try in the opposite direction. But, what use? Better to spend my last strength remembering what was good in existence.

Wait . . . What was that, pressed against the wall by the wind, yonder to the right? An undulant mass – darva? No, but perhaps distantly related. Theor went over for a look.

He found a tough, ragged-edged sheet, roughly square, about twenty feet on a side. A man would have called it blue, in the minute before Earthly temperatures turned the labile molecules of Jovian life into ash. Theor saw it as black. The shape was not ordinarily flat as now, when it was moulded onto the rock face. Several thick, fuzzy strands ran from the corners to a thing that resembled a good-sized, wart-covered log. When Theor hefted that, he found it nearly as heavy as himself.

Bit by painstaking bit, he worked out what the organism must be. Normally it drifted about like an open bag. The upper surface absorbed energy, the cilia took up ammonia and minerals from the clouds. There was a nice balance between the parachute effect of the leaf and the weight of the lumpish object dangling below. It must be a druga species, alternating between vegetable and animal, currently encysted while metamorphosis went on.

He tried to cut open the shell – there was meat inside! – but it resisted both his knife and the hardest blows he could deliver with a stone. Well, at least he could try to make a

118

star-shape catching bag out of the leaf; and it could double as a blanket. He had been cold so long that only the prospect of a little shelter reminded him that he was.

A gust caught the parachute. Theor hauled it down and stood on it, barely in time to keep it from blowing away. It had tugged so strongly that he almost failed. *Hang on to your luck! There is a balance of fortune, after all, as I daresay the laws of chance predict. This cliff which stops me has also stopped a thing of service.*

– *Wait!*

Thundersmitten by his vision Theor hugged an upward-flying edge of the sheet against his thorax. So terrifying was the thought that he almost surrendered then and there. But he had ridden forgars in the past. Now, from some memory of Leenant and Pors, he drew the will he needed.

Quick, before panic paralyses me.

The knife shook in his hand as he sawed at the fibres. One by one they parted, bleeding stickily. Without the weight of the cocoon, the leaf slatted crazily. Theor had to fight it off his face, again and again, as he tied the strands about himself. When at length he stepped off, the sheet billowed up and he was nearly dragged off his feet.

Not quite. He had some net weight. So little, however, that he should be able to go down the cliff. It looked like being as hazardous a thing as he had ever attempted. But the alternative was surely death, and strange sky-fish nuzzling his bones.

He took his courage in both hands and lowered himself over the edge.

At first he skidded wildly on a glass-smooth slope, legs flailing, the leaf bucking and swooping at his rear. If that drogue collapsed, he would slide free, faster and faster until he smashed against some crag, which might or might not be merciful enough to kill him instantly. He grabbed the forward lines and hauled to belly out the sheet. The cords bit into his stomach, he slowed, he was almost dancing . . .

The mountain dropped away beneath him. His feet trod air.

Fraser could have told him about thermal updraughts. Theor had only slight knowledge of them; they were a weak and infrequent phenomenon in his home depths. Here, with less pressure and density and more temperature gradient, they were able to develop enormous thrust.

Fraser was lost to Theor. The Jovian knew simply and terrifyingly that a force had seized him. He dangled in the whirling clouds, strangling as the air grew yet thinner, whipped away and away into emptiness.

14

Was that ringing only in his head, on his final tumble into night?

No. There were shapes around him. They wove in and out of the ammonia smoke, quick shadows with wings, barely glimpsed before they vanished again. Their flutings and chimings blended with the boom of wind, the thrum of the cords that bound him.

He didn't know how long he had been carried, half-conscious, through the sky. But slowly a little strength and awareness returned. The air current was bending downward and carrying him with it on a long curve.

Abruptly he broke out of the clouds. The sun's infrared blazed low at his back in an immense dark vault. Never before had he seen the actual, blinding disc. Its rays slanted across billowy masses scattered beneath him, throwing umbras and penumbras over their red heights, bursting into a circular rainbow where ice crystals refracted radiance. Far below he saw land, a rugged grey reach of mountains giving way to a million shades of lilla and pirell-brown in the east where the Rollarikan forests began. He could even identify a volcano at work down there, a crimson-tinged blotch near the border of vision.

He swivelled his head and looked around him with dazed eyes. The flying creatures swooped near. They numbered perhaps a score − about three feet of slender, fluke-tailed body, broad membranous wings, two legs with grasping-toed feet drawn up under the abdomen, sharp-nosed heads at the end of curving necks. Their eyes were smaller than his, but they had arms ending in hands with opposable thumbs.

Some carried ropes and some had harpoons.

The Hidden Folk, he knew. *So they are not a legend.* He waited helplessly for whatever they would do to him.

They gambolled and curvetted, crying to each other. The notes came from their mouths, they lacked throat pouches and gills. *Evidently they breathe like humans. (Mark, Mark, how are you faring?) But then, if the human doctrine of evolution is true, they are incredibly far removed from me, not even the same phylum. How many million years ago did a few of the animalcules that were our common ancestors drift up . . . or down?*

For a time he hoped they would simply let him descend. But a decision was reached. Lariats snaked out. In the face of their weapons, he did not resist the loops that closed around forelegs and torso. The flyers dragged him off, half aided and half hampered by the parachute.

Their ropes cut cruelly into his flesh. Wings beat the air hard and he heard the breath become rapid, in and out of the lungs of his captors. He tried to relax until a chance should come to – to do what?

The ocean behind him drank down the sun. Some light remained, glimmering eldritch from the upper surfaces of the clouds. Fraser had spoken of phosphorescence effects, once.

Presently a brighter gleam hove into view. The flyers made for it. One went ahead, and came back with a flitting ghostly swarm of his fellows. Their voices sang through the stillness that had fallen.

Tired though he was, Theor exclaimed aloud when he saw the destination clearly. It was a mass of small, blowing bubbles, riding free in the air, a hundred thick and half a mile in diameter. Shallow depressions pocked it overall, and shapes stirred in them; they were nests.

He was brought down to one on the perimeter. The surface yielded a little beneath him, and no doubt the whole community sank ever so slightly when his weight was added. Several harpoons pointed at him while a couple of the creatures removed the ropes and his parachute. A cord was run between his neck and right foreleg. He grinned a bit. Did they think he would try to escape?

The other Hidden Folk fluttered about, piping to each other. He thought of talking back, but the effort was too much. *Let me only sleep. I am so tired.* Uncaring what they did to him, he hung his head and closed his eyes.

Dawn roused him. For a space he nictitated stupidly, trying to remember what had happened. The knowledge returned in pieces, none seeming very real.

Yet here he was!

He moved stiffly, hampered by the cord, till he peered over the rim of the nest. A mile beneath him, Rollarik streamed with morning fog. He could see the Steeps of Jonnary to the south, running east to join the Wilderwall. Not far north of that, the volcano spouted, isolated from the ranges, forest carpeting its feet. Everything was tiny at this distance, blurred, and unattainable.

The bubble-mass bobbed gently in a low wind. Clouds blew past, torn off the huge bank that perpetually darkened the west. The Hidden Folk were about their business. He could see what he took to be females and young at work in other nests, spreading strips of meat out to dry, husking the fruits of aerial vegetation, spinning cord between their hands. What containers they had were basket-woven. Tools were chipped from light, brittle bone. The male (?) who perched alertly near Theor was armed with a harpoon which the Nyarran could now study in detail. Its staff was painstakingly spliced together from bone sections; the head was a tusk from some animal.

'So you are hunters,' Theor murmured aloud. Starved for

air as well as food, he still felt slow-brained. But his rest had given back some strength. 'Poorer savages, even, than the woodsrunners down there. But of course you have no minerals, nothing but those life forms which float at your level.'

This town was a considerable achievement, though. Probably the bubbles were bladders that upheld some variety of plant. A natural congeries wouldn't be anywhere near this big. The labour of generations must have gone to assembling so many. What stuck them together – a glue?

His attention returned to the cord that handicapped him. They had left his knife in the sheath, either not recognising what it was or failing to notice it in the dark. He could easily cut himself free. The reason for his binding might be simple caution, or something worse.

A twitter wheeled him around. Two more males had landed on the rim of the nest beside the guard. They also carried harpoons. For a minute he stared into their bright strange eyes, and remembered those tales that were muttered at night about the Hidden Folk.

'Greeting to you,' he ventured. There was no response. He tried every language of which he had any smattering. They perched where they were, their wings rippled but no words came from the beaky heads.

Well, he might have anticipated as much. Contact between their race and his amounted to fleeting, accidental glimpses. No doubt only a rare disaster forced his kind down to the heat, murk, and chokingly thick air of ground level. Maybe those who were so forced never got back alive to the sky where they belonged.

Music ran between the three on the rim. Their weapons lifted.

Theor sprang back, stumbled on the rope, and fell. 'No!' he roared. 'Why did you bring me here, if you will kill me now?'

The answer was chillingly plain. While he wore the parachute, he was transportable.

'Are you Ulunt-Khazul, to devour a being that thinks?'

How can they know I do?

The realisation might not have come to Theor in time, or at all, had there been no history of contact between Nyarr and Ganymede. It flashed through him how long and difficult the initial stages had been, before anyone so much as understood that the noises from the sky-stone were meant as signals; and how little the Hidden Folk knew about Jupiter's surface, hardly more than the humans did, no, probably much less . . .

He whipped out his knife and slashed the rope across. The harpooners stopped, astounded, almost in the act of casting their shafts. Theor got to his feet, lifted the knife in one hand and held the other hand above his head, open so they would notice the fingers.

'I am your kin,' he said, forming each syllable with vast care. 'These are words I speak, not beast cries.'

Tableau, in that nest above the world. Theor dared not move. If he alarmed them, he might well get those teeth between his ribs – for he was so big and heavy, so potentially damaging, that he wondered why they had not butchered him in his sleep, or immediately on arrival here. Well, as for the latter, they must have wanted time to decide what to do. And once they did agree to kill him, they might well have wanted daylight to see what they were at. Since they were used to the painful brightness at this altitude, the soft luminance of their own home might not register on their senses.

Theor pointed to the belt around his torso, the disc on his breast. 'Would a mere animal carry such as this?' he pleaded. 'How could a dumb brute tie itself to that leaf?'

Well, they may have guessed that I have an owner. Or perhaps, like the Rollarikans, they draw little distinction between themselves and the rest of creation, and would not be too surpised if a beast acted somewhat like a thinker.

A flyer pointed his beak at him and whistled some notes. Theor grimaced. 'I could not come near imitating your sounds, my friend. But . . . let me see. The humans began by sending clicks that were arithmetical sums. I do not think that would convey much to you. However – '

He cut the divided rope entirely off him, sheathed the knife, and began to tie knots. Erelong one of the flyers hopped closer to watch. Theor went through square knot, bowline, sheet bend, and still more elaborate configurations. He finished with a Turk's head and tossed the rope over. The Hidden Folk shot into the air in alarm. Theor stood quiet, unsure how much longer he had to live. When no harpoons rammed into him, he pointed at his mouth.

They grasped that. One fluttered off, returning with a piece of flesh and several pulpy spheroids. He threw them down to Theor, who took care to eat with good manners. The round objects contained juice that somewhat quenched his thirst. He guessed that no animals here drank as he did. What would they drink from? Most likely their food supplied ammonia, if they did not absorb it while travelling through clouds.

Two remained on guard on the rim, but the third came down and began making signs. Theor responded. He got across that he belonged on the surface, which occasioned no little surprise. 'You really have no idea about the ground, do you, except for what you can see,' he remarked. 'A few myths, maybe.' He pointed to himself and then to the volcano. 'Do you understand? I want to be taken there.' It was a vantage point from which he might conceivably spy Walfilo's people. Nothing else suggested itself.

After several repetitions, the being seemed to get the idea. He recoiled. Well, the trip was dangerous for his kind. Why should they do their prisoner such a favour?

Theor took his knife out again and demonstrated how well it cut. He had noticed nothing in this community that had a real edge. More signs: take me there and this is yours.

A hunter on the rim made a vicious gesture with his spear. Theor read the meaning plainly: why shouldn't we simply kill you and take the thing?

He rushed forward, away from the others, climbed the rubbery bowl, and settled himself on the edge. He didn't dare look over from this position, but he put the knife back and said, 'If I die now, I'll fall, and this will fall with me. I think my body would rip through any net you can place beneath.'

The beings piped among themselves. Finally one flew off. Theor made himself as comfortable as he could. It might be a long wait.

The time was shorter than expected, though. The sun did not yet stand at noon when a score or so of the winged ones returned. They soared overhead in a silence that said much to Theor. When two entered the nest, dragging his parachute behind them, he knew that this was either a ruse to get him helpless, or a victory.

'I can only assume you have honour,' he said, accepted the strands and secured them around himself. The nearest hunter pointed to his knife. Theor pointed firmly to the volcano. The creature sighed.

Theor stepped off the edge.

The withes slammed into his abdomen. He groaned with pain. It eased, and he was on his way down. To and fro he swung, hearing the wind whistle past him. A hunter tossed him a rope. He caught hold. The Hidden Folk lined themselves along the far end and started off.

The great nest was soon lost to view. It was not surprising that no ground dweller had ever seen one like that, or an aerial pasture, or the monsters which browsed there. A mile up, with half the atmosphere and a goodly percentage of the clouds between, they would be invisible. He wondered what other strangenesses dwelt in his heaven.

After a while he felt the strain increase on his tow rope, until at last he could hold it no more and must knot it about his waist. The hunters were plainly labouring hard. He needed a few minutes to deduce the reason. Nature had meant the leaf which supported him to float at a certain altitude. He was now down to where the air was getting appreciably denser. His gills recognised that; he felt how sluggishness and cold evaporated from him. Carefully, he heaved on the lines, spilling wind from the parachute to ease the back pressure.

One by one, several of those who drew him let go and disappeared upward. They couldn't stand these conditions. He had a dreadful instant of thinking that he would never touch soil alive.

But the rest persisted. *What a treasure that blade must be to them! As if I should dive to the bottom of the ocean to get some jewel.* Of course, the doubled hydrogen content lent them extra energy, but he could imagine how it must scorch their throats. *And still they keep their pledge. I hope someday, somehow, we can meet them again and give them our help.*

And now the volcano loomed ahead. The cone was not very high, but he saw the crater as an immense incandescence, and a lesser firepool halfway down the slope. A pillar of smoke, organic material disintegrated by the heat, stood above, climbing and climbing until it mingled with low rainclouds. Lightning flickered to the east. He heard the forest sough beneath him. A gust brought him such fumes that he clapped his hands over his stung antennae. His companions wailed. To them, this might be absolute night, relieved only by the red reflections off the mountain's breath.

The ground rushed to meet him. He struck with bent legs,

128

rolled over, and got up. Trees gloomed around him. The little hunters circled blind and cheeping in the air.

He cut himself loose from the parachute. It blew quickly away. How simple to vanish into the woods! And surely he, alone in a barbarian country, needed a knife more than anyone . . . 'Here I am!' he bawled. 'Ulloala, here!'

A flyer came to earth and stood huddled in his wings. Theor walked over, took off the sheathed weapon, and closed the thin fingers around its handle. 'Farewell, mind-brother,' he said.

The being whistled and rose. His fellows blundered near. They began to climb, more slowly than Theor had expected. *But wait, yes, Mark has told me of decompression effects. They have a long journey before they see the sun once more.* He stood and watched until the last of the Hidden Folk was gone from sight.

15

As he looked more carefully at his surroundings, Theor felt a return of dismay.

He stood on the edge of forest growth. The trees were mostly yorwar, thick-boled, with hollow upward-floating limbs and the characteristic Jovian leafage which would have reminded a man of lung tissue. Their 'photosynthesis,' building complex molecules out of methane and ammonia, releasing hydrogen in the process, depended on synchrotron radiation as well as lightning and the feeble sun, and so required a maximisation of internal surface. The crowns rarely lifted more than fifteen feet about the roots. But they stretched endlessly on, farther than he could see, and Walfilo might be almost anywhere in those reaches.

Ahead of him, the volcano reared dark against the flicker in the slowly approaching storm. Infrared light glanced off the smoke that poured from its crater, struck the naked ice of the mountain and shimmered. He heard the thing rumble, and felt the deep ground vibrations through his bones. He was not unfamiliar with naturel firepots, he had helped cast implements over some of them in Ath. But that had been in a smithy, surrounded by tools and tradition, with a dozen fellow beings to help. Now he was awesomely alone.

And unarmed. *That* had better be remedied at once. He climbed onto the slope and pawed about in the debris until he found a suitable pair of rocks. Chemically, they were water crystallised together with a small amount of silicon and magnesium compounds. But they fractured like obsidian. He quickly struck out a *coup de poing* and several

130

spearheads. Returning to the woods, he used the hand-axe to gnaw a fairly straight shaft off a larrik bush, and secured one of the points to this with a strip cut from the fibrous interior of the plant. The spares he wrapped in a leaf and slung at his belt. His weapons were cruder than any belonging to a local barbarian – those tribes had not lost skill in this art as had the civilised peoples to some degree – but he felt a good deal happier for them.

Now food. His last meal was already long behind him.

Perhaps his luck had turned. He cast about for less than an hour before coming upon the fresh track of a skalpad. A while he hesitated. That was a formidable thing to attack, even with a good lance and fresh muscles. But there was a lot of food there.

Also ... He clapped his hands together. An idea had come to him.

Excitement thuttered in his veins. He suppressed it. ' "One step at a time," said the snakefish as he went ashore,' he cautioned himself. His voice was so small against the steadily rising wind and nearing thunder that he fell silent and concentrated on following the trail.

It debouched in a meadow. The skalpad was feeding. Even through the troubled air, Theor could hear the crunch of jaws and see the bushes ripple outward, wavelike, from the great domed shell that heaved above them. He circled until he faced the animal, took a firm two-handed grip on his spear, and charged.

The armoured neck lifted, tendrils drew back and the hooked mouth gaped. Six thick legs waddled to meet the attack. The earth quivered beneath a bulk more than twice Theor's.

'Kee-*yi!*' At the last second, he shifted his aim toward the vulnerable throat pouch. With all his weight and speed behind it, the spear drove through.

The skalpad twisted around. Theor barely dodged a bite

131

that could have taken off an arm. The head shook, the embedded shaft splintered against the soil, blood pumped out over the scrub. Theor believed the wound was mortal, but night was approaching even faster than the rain. He couldn't wait much longer. Unwrapping his bundle, he took the axe in one hand and a point in the other. The rest he held in his mouth. He raced around the threshing monster, came alongside, and drove the daggerlike spearhead into one eye. His next several passes missed, when he must duck from the snapping jaws. When nothing remained but the hand-axe, he charged again and again, striking when he could. It was a savage business. He felt nearly as tired and sick as his prey when the skalpad's limbs finally buckled.

But there was no time for guilt, if he was to take advantage of the weather. Light was already draining out of the west, too. He assaulted the body with the cutting edges of his *coup de poing*, not stopping to do a good butcher's job, concerned only to get the shell off and some pounds of meat for himself. Let the scavengers have the rest. Wings rattled overhead and howling went among the trees.

When roughly cleaned out, the shell could be rolled. Otherwise he would never have gotten it over those dark, tangled miles back to the volcano, let alone up the slope. After the mountains he had traversed, this wasn't any climb to speak of. But he was shaking with exhaustion by the time he reached the secondary vent halfway between foot and peak.

By then, also, the first rain was upon him. Heavy drops of ammonia lashed his skin, and the low cloud roof was almost continuously lit by lightning. Where it struck the firepot, the rain hissed back in steam, so that Theor entered white billows of fog in which danced tiny sparks.

The vapour offered some protection, however, against the heat that radiated from the vent. When he looked into that yard-wide hole, his eyes were dazzled. The roaring down there was as loud as the thunder around him. His gills cramped shut in reflexive protest against the fumes; again and again he must retreat for air.

The moltenness which raged within was water, and its temperature was only a few hundred degrees Fahrenheit. But Theor's kind of life had not evolved to endure such conditions.

And in truth the forces which brought them about were stupendous. The metallic core of Jupiter is wrapped in thousands of miles of solid hydrogen. Above this is a shell of ice, less vast but quite adequate to maintain pressures that collapse ordinary molecular structures. Somewhere in those depths an equilibrium had been broken. The pressure in a certain volume dropped below a critical value. A titanic mass of ice changed to a less dense crystalline phase in an explosion comparable to that of a large thermonuclear bomb. Liquefied by the released energy, water spurted through the riven planetary surface. It could not vapourise. the atmosphere weighed too heavily on it. Cooling and congealing, it built up a cone which rapidly grew to be a mountain. The flow might continue for centuries before a new balance was struck and the volcano became extinct.

Slowly, painfully, Theor built a wall of stones on the lower lip of the vent, until he had a roughly level rim around it. He spent nearly his last strength getting the skalpad shell up on top, inverted to the sky.

Now he could only wait. He found shelter beneath an overhang further down and tore a haunch of meat with his teeth. The rawness meant nothing to him. Cooking was still a highly experimental art, indulged in by a few Ath folk who had ready access to heat. But he missed the spices and the tenderizing enzyme juices of home.

Home . . . did it still exist?

He huddled back and waited. The rain brawled on. Well, the longer and heavier the fall, the better for him. He had thought he might need several storms, but perhaps this one would do. He slept.

The rain continued through the night and day and night, on into the following morning. A human would not have been able to comprehend the Noachian magnitude of precipitation; but it was not unusual for Jupiter, which is constructed on another scale than Earth. When at length the fog that followed it had lifted, Theor emerged. He felt physically better and more hopeful than at any time since Gillen Beach. Still, his pulses racketed as he dragged the skalpad shell off the firepot with a stone chipped into a sort of hook. Its hard substance was blackened and shrunken, but the bowl was still intact and struck the ground with a crash. Eagerly, Theor peered inside.

Several pounds of metal glistened on the bottom.

He was careful to wrap his hands in leaves before taking the cooled lumps forth. It was unpredictable what the stuff might do to him in such a quantity, even though he was adapted to breathing it and probably used it in his metabolism. Fraser had told him how tricky raw sodium could be.

The man had also explained that this element, dissolved by ammonia and forming complexes with it, was what supplied many of the cloud colours. And it reacted powerfully with liquid water. Perhaps that explained certain disasters in the early days of hydrurgy. For when you boiled away the ammonia –

The rest of Theor's day went to climb the mountain and erect a wall on the southeast verge of the crater. He stared often in that direction – Walfilo's host must be somewhere yonder, if they yet lived – but saw only forest and the remote Wilderwall. This land was so big that an army was swallowed without trace.

Night fell. He glanced at the seething below, summoned his courage, wrenched loose a gob of the soft metal and threw it over the edge.

His dive for shelter was barely fast enough. Fire vomited, water drops pelted his barricade, the volcano smoke was lit yellow. He could not see that colour, his eyes registered a lurid pirell, but he felt the radiation beat on his skin. Echoes snapped back and forth until his head tolled.

When the explosion was over, he cast a second piece. And a third. Wait several beats; then a fourth and fifth in quick succession. He had duplicated in light the call for help of a military drummer.

He had only sufficient material to repeat the cycle once. And then he could only wait. Reflected off clouds, the flashes were so brilliant to Jovian vision that they should be perceptible for fifty miles or better. But were his people that close? And would they investigate? He crept tiredly back to his shelter.

Footfalls roused him some hours after dawn.

Two males were climbing the mountain. They were gaunt and dirty, but they carried Nyarran weapons. And when they saw him they burst into a gallop.

'Reeve, oh, my Reeve!'

Theor embraced them. For a space he was joyous, he had beaten the wilderness, reached his own kind by a road no Jovian ever trod before. Then he thought, *The real fight is only begun,* and said, 'We had best start back at once. This is not a good country.'

The scouts had come on forgarback, with a couple of remounts. Before turning one over to Theor, they brought him up to date on what had happened. 'Though little there is to tell, Reeve. We could not make a stand anywhere on the plain, so we crossed the Steeps and went on for two days north, to where there is a lake and game can be gotten. There we are still encamped, not knowing whether to return and die or stay and become Rollarikans. Some have argued that we could swing far east of Medalon and so south until we reached the Foresters, who might aid us. But doubtful that is, and our homeland would long have fallen to the enemy before we could prepare an expedition.'

'Yes, we have little time,' Theor agreed. 'Nyarr cannot stand siege much longer than foodstores last, and they are scant at this season. Without Nyarr city and the ice works of Ath, even if we won back the land we would be meat for the next barbarian incursion.'

He pondered what to do as they travelled. There was no clear answer. But his resolution stiffened, and he entered the camp with long strides.

It was not conspicuous. The plaited lean-tos were scattered through the woods and most of the people were out each day on the chase. But Walfilo had had a large hut erected on the lakeshore, and his banner flew above.

The scarred professional welcomed Theor with a genuine gladness, heard his story and was gratifyingly impressed. But then he asked, 'What have you in mind to do?'

'Return as fast as we can,' Theor answered. 'If we cross the Wilderwall at Windgate Pass, we will enter Medalon not far from the Brantor River, with forests close by for the making of rafts. Thus we can approach the city with speed, unobserved until we are near – at which time we will go ashore and attack the Ulunt-Khazul. When those within sally forth, the enemy will be caught between two hosts.'

'Which he will chop into bits,' Walfilo grunted. 'We are not the army which your demi-fathers led out. Death, wounds, and hunger have dealt hardly with us.'

'What other choice have we?'

'This. We are settling into Rollarik, already learning its ways, having daily more success at winning food. No band of miserable woodsrunners can oppose us. Belike we can even raise a smithy on that volcano where you were, and so continue to have cast weapons. We can establish ourselves as the germ of a new nation.'

'Leaving our kin to be devoured?'

Walfilo winced. 'That is a hard necessity. But I have been a fighter all my life, Reeve. This is not the first time I have had to sacrifice much in order to keep something vital. A march against the Ulunt-Khazul can only end in us too being devoured; and then darkness will indeed fall over the world.'

'You may know more of war than I do,' Theor said angrily, 'but you show little knowledge of what is needed for a civilisation. Why do the Rollarikans forever seek to spill across Medalon? Because this country is poor. Rains leach the soil until only trees as hardy as the yorwar flourish. The plants that supply most of our fibre would not grow here. And do you know how many octads of years it would take to clear enough land for even the scantiest ranching? As for that volcano, the ice minerals I have seen there are not those which make good alloys. We are too few to maintain a literate culture – and how much help would mates be that we stole from the barbarians? I tell you, if we remain here the darkness will come almost as fast, and even more surely, than if we go home and hazard our lives.'

'That is your judgement. Mine is otherwise. We might in time regain Medalon, you know, by the help of allies – '

'A Medalon ruined, with its people dead or scattered or enslaved, because we were too cowardly to help them!'

Walfilo's comb bristled. 'Call me not coward,' he said, 'or I will cease to call you Reeve.'

Theor choked off his own wrath. An inbred coolness descended; he weighed the problem, watched the balance tilt, and said: 'I take it you forbid a return.' Walfilo gestured yes. 'Let us assemble the army, then, so that they may understand the case.'

He spent the remainder of the day preparing his speech. His education had included rhetoric, and his conversations with the alien Fraser had sharpened that training.

Toward sunset the host gathered by the lake. Theor mounted a tree stump and looked over them. Spears and helmets blazed in the last light, rank upon rank; the shields were faded and battered, but he could still make out emblems which had a proud history.

'Males and demimales of Nyarr.' His voice rolled into a deep, waiting stillness, where the forest stood black above the lake's glimmer. The least stirring went through the armed lines, like a small gust before a storm. 'Both my demi-fathers died at Gillen Beach, where you also left comrades and kin. Now I am told I must betray them.'

'What?' Walfilo started furiously. 'I deny –'

'The Reeve is speaking,' Theor said. 'By the law of Nyarr, you shall say what you will afterward; but none now may interrupt.' He turned back to the army. 'The enemy has pillaged his way to our city. He seals it shut with edged ice, and waits for our children and mates to die. I cannot call that an evil thing to do – not yet – not while we are doing just the same.'

They roared!

When Theor had finished, Walfilo took the stump, looked coldly at the weapons which threatened him, and cried, 'If this is your will, so be it. We shall spend two or three more days gathering food, and then we return to Medalon. Dismissed!'

He stepped down again and sought Theor. 'That was a cruel and unfair word you gave them,' he said through the shouting. 'You knew well that I was acting as seemed best for the people.'

'Indeed I do.' Theor clasped the warrior's shoulder. 'But had I not the same obligation? You told me yourself, often one must sacrifice much in order to keep something vital.'

'So my honour is the sacrifice.'

'No, never. They won't recall my words against you. Not very long. What will live is the fact that you led us home.'

Walfilo stood a while in the twilight regarding the younger male. Finally he laid his axe at Theor's feet, the ancient sign of obedience. 'Indeed the blood of your folk is in you,' he said, 'and you are a Reeve born.' Teeth flashed in a smile. 'And thank you! My decision was nigh too heavy for me to bear. You have lifted it onto your own back. I will die sooner, following your counsel, but much more gladly.'

16

Fraser laid down his wrench. 'That's that,' he said. 'No more safety cut-off on this engine. Now we only have to start her.'

He rose, awkward in his suit, and found himself confronting Lorraine. The flashtube she had held for him, to furnish light, wavered in her hand, making grotesque shadows chase across the room, over crowded machines and dully gleaming bulkheads. There the undiffused puddle of glow was reflected. Behind the faceplate, her features stood forth against the darkness in the doorway, and the gold hair seemed almost to crackle with the cold that filled the moonship.

'Well,' he said, wishing he had better words, 'let's go.'

'Mark – '

'What?'

'Oh . . . nothing, I guess,' Her eyelids fluttered down. He could see how she braced herself. 'I just wanted to say . . . if we don't make it . . . you've been a grand guy. There's nobody I'd rather be with now.'

Despite the synthetic emotional control he had eaten, his heart sprang. He patted her hand, fabric to fabric. 'Same to you, kid. I'll even admit – I think you'll understand – I had a tough time remaining a gentleman, all those cycles in your apartment. I might not have managed it with someone I thought less of.'

'Hell, you think I wasn't having trouble being a lady?' She turned on her heel. 'C'mon.'

They climbed the ladder to the control room. Fraser set the engine to warmup and threw the starter switch. The preliminary whine shivered through his boots.

'Quick before the fusion starts!'

She hung back at the airlock, as if to let him go first. He shoved her ahead. The vibration built up with unnatural speed and raggedness. When he was halfway down the accommodation ladder, he jumped the rest of the distance.

Blind in the gloom between the parked vessels, he fumbled around after her. Fingers closed on his arm. She led him to the north end of the area, and around westward.

Cautiously, he peered from behind a landing jack. The field stretched yellowish grey between him and the town, in the light of third-quarter Jupiter. Ahead and to his right stood the *Olympia,* his entire hope. But his gaze was held on the enormous spheroid of the *Vega,* on the guns silhouetted lean against the Milky Way and the dozen armed men ringing her in. *Another minute, I'd guess, till that engine blows.* As if his estimate were exact, he counted down. *Fifty-nine, fifty-eight, fifty-six, no, seven, fifty-five . . . twenty-four, twenty-three, twenty-two —*

The world shuddered beneath him. A roar passed through his feet and hammered in his skull. The ship beside him reeled on her jacks. He knew better than to look at the fire which spouted upward, but he saw its light pitiless on the ground, blue-white, making each rock beyond the concrete apron stand forth like a mountain.

A crack opened in the field and ran zigzag toward the blind safety wall before Aurora. A moonship on the south side swayed, tottered, and fell with infinite slowness, struck at last and made the ground ring with her metal anguish. Vapour boiled through the space she had occupied, hellishly tinted by the fire.

The chaos endured for one split instant, then the reactor was destroyed and the reaction ended. Night came again. Jupiter looked wan and the stunned eye could make out not a single star.

Fraser and Lorraine ran.

They didn't pause to see if they were noticed. A shot would tell them that. In long frantic bounds they crossed the open field, reached the *Olympia,* and skidded to a halt.

Because she was meant to land aerodynamically on unknown and possibly unsafe terrain, in a strong gravitational field, she rested on wheeled jacks, and horizontally rather than vertically. Hence the cargo entry was lower than for a regular spaceship – but nonetheless higher than was convenient. Fraser braced his hands against the support below the hatch. Lorraine sprang onto his shoulders, reached up, and spun the manual control. A circle opened. She chinned herself through, flopped down, and extended a hand. Fraser jumped to catch her. Briefly, he was afraid she would be dragged out by his weight. But she drew him in, he rolled over, bounced to his feet, and pelted for the pilot room. She closed the hatch and followed.

An equally massive door guarded the human part of the ship. Fraser cranked the wheel and cursed its gear ratio. Through! He entered the forward section and plunked himself down in the pilot's seat. The board was as dark as the rest of the vessel, and laid out differently from those he was used to. He was helpless until Lorraine came behind him and aimed the flashtube at his hands.

'That's better,' he panted. When he could see the layout, it was familiar. It ought to be. He'd spent hours memorising the diagrams she smuggled to him, the instructions and specifications. After so much mental rehearsal, the act had a tinge of falsity.

A throbbing awoke, the hull transmitted it to him and he leaned back with a whistle. Sweat coursed past his brows and stung his eyes. Ten minutes for warmup – that was cutting matters pretty fine, but he dared wait no longer than he must.

There were no ports in this ship, and he didn't want to risk activating the viewscreens before he was ready to lift.

Someone might be sniffing around outside with a detector. 'What're they doing, do you think?' he asked inanely.

'Running around like beheaded chickens, I'll bet,' she answered. 'They'll come to order fast, they've got tight discipline, but right now I'd love to watch the confusion.'

He leaned over to assist her into the harness of the chair beside his. 'Well,' he said, 'so far it went like the proverbial clockwork. I wouldn't be surprised but that the whole operation will succeed. How are you going to like being a heroine?'

She forced lightness into her tone. 'As much as you're going to like being a hero. Which is to say, plenty.'

'Uh, I dunno. No more privacy, no more daring to indulge in little human fallings from virtue – God, I'll bet I wind up addressing a Rotarian lunch! It's different for you, of course. You can enjoy the glamour aspect. But I'm too old and homely.'

Her look lingered on him, in the dim shadow-haunted light. 'You're not old, Mark,' she said low.

'You don't deny the homeliness, eh?' he tried to chuckle.

'*I'm* old enough not to care for boys. I prefer men. And you're more a man, in every way, than anybody else I ever met.' She drew a quick breath. 'Oh, dear,' she said confusedly, 'we're not getting this harness fastened at all.'

They fell into silence.

The engine rumble strengthened. 'Time!' said Fraser. He switched on interior lights and viewscreens.

It was as if suddenly he commanded a tower above the field. Men swarmed about in an antlike orderliness. Those working by the moonships wore bulky radiation armour. A 'dozer had already arrived and started heaping a protective ringwall. 'Swayne's even sharper than I thought,' said Lorraine grudgingly.

'Damn!' Fraser said. 'Our blast'll incinerate those guys yonder, the ones closest to us.'

'Do you care? – Yes, you would. I guess we can spend thirty seconds' worth of warning time.'

Fraser flipped the radio to the general communication band and plugged in a jack to his helmet set. 'Attention, all personnel,' he droned. 'Your attention out there! Spaceship *Olympia* about to lift. Clear the area. Clear the area.'

A voice screamed back: 'What the hell is this?' But Fraser was watching the *Vega*. He saw a turret swing about, readying to shoot as soon as he went beyond the minimum radius.

'You've got ten more seconds to get away,' he called.

They ran. Two men came nearer, though, stopped at the very edge of the danger zone and raised their laser guns. *They've got guts, for sure,* Fraser thought, and pulled the main switch.

The surge of power clattered the teeth in his jaws. He saw the exhaust cloud spreading below him, like snow tongued with fire, out across the field. Even by conduction, the noise invaded his entire being. Steering jets blasted as the jacks withdrew. The ship's nose swung sickeningly upward. Acceleration struck. The field fell away.

Ganymede fell away. It was a pocked and pitted crescent below him, and the sun rose over the eastern rim.

Fraser cut the thrust when he had twice escape velocity and returned his chair to the upright position. Free fall was stillness and dream, with stars crowding the spaceward screen, but he was too busy to notice. 'Run me a radar beam back that way, Lory, I want to make sure we aren't being followed.'

'We can't be. Every one of their boats is tied up in orbit around the other moons, or out toward the asteroids. And we can outrun the *Vega*.'

'We can't outrun a missile,' he said bleakly. 'I've got to bring us down at Blocksberg undetected, remember?'

Her fingers danced over the console. The screen came

144

aglow. A computer threw figures onto a set of meters and drew two continuously changing curves on a fluorescent dial.

'A couple of rifle shells,' she deduced. 'They aren't on a collision orbit with us, though.'

'Whew! That's a relief. Not that we couldn't evade them, at this distance, but I was worried that Traffic Control might have managed to slap a radar beam on us. Now our angular diameter is too small for them to have any real chance of doing so. I'll swing us around behind Jupe. By the time we orbit back here, everything should have settled down and we can make a quick sneak landing.'

Without navigation tables or equipment to give him information more precise than memory and trained vision supplied, he could only calculate approximate vectors. They would serve, though, for his rough purposes. He set the panel and applied one-tenth gee acceleration. More than that, and the exhaust would be detectable at too long a range. He'd speed up when they'd put a hundred kilomiles or so between themselves and Ganymede.

The receiver blinked a red signal. 'Oh, oh,' Lorraine said. 'Callers. Think they've locked onto us?'

'No. They're broadcasting. I may as well reply. They aren't set up to triangulate on us.' Fraser plugged his radio connection back in.

'Attention, spaceship *Olympia*!'

'Swayne's voice,' Lorraine whispered. He saw fear touch her face.

That roused anger in him. '*Olympia* speaking,' he snapped. 'What the devil do you want?'

'I might ask the same,' Swayne answered dryly, 'as well as who's aboard. This is the commandant of the military administration.'

'Nu?' Fraser decided not to admit his or Lorraine's identity: partly out of contrariness, partly to avoid reprisals on his family. Of course, they'd soon guess hers . . .

'Return at once, in the name of the law.'

'If that's all you've got to say, over and out.'

'Wait. I know what you're after. It's obvious. You think you can make Earth. You can't. That ship isn't supplied. You can't have carried along enough to make any difference. A spaceship's water recycler needs a certain minimum quantity to function. You haven't even any air.'

'I'm breathing yet.'

'You know as well as I do that the cycler in a spacesuit is different from the powered system in a ship . . . which also requires a certain pressure to work. Your chemicals will be used up in a matter of days.'

'If you're trying to scare me, you're wasting air yourself. Let me scare you instead. When the Navy arrives, you'll be held to account for everything that's happened in the Jovian System. Think that over and conduct yourself accordingly.'

'Shut up,' Swayne said. 'Do you believe I'm such an idiot as you? You must have arranged to get supplies somewhere. I doubt very much if it's at one of the other moons. How could there be secret communication between them? But in case that is your aim, then, for your information, each has a boat on orbital radar picket, and each boat will get radio orders to fire at sight of you.'

Uh-huh. That's why you can't keep watch on all Ganymede.

'I think you must plan to come back to some part of this moon,' Swayne said. 'I've thought for some time, in any event, that we need a close-in patrol as an added precaution. So . . . a number of moonships are promptly going to take up stations. They aren't well equipped for such work – they will be when we get their radars rebuilt – but meanwhile they can keep every square foot of the surface under visual observation. If you land anywhere on Ganymede, you'll be seen. The *Vega* will scramble and blast you. She can do that

146

on a few seconds' notice if she's kept on continuous full alert, warmed up. And that's what she will be until I'm certain you've been taken care of.'

'Oh, no, no, no,' Lorraine gasped. The colour bleached from her skin.

It was as if a boot had struck Fraser in the groin. But somehow he snarled, 'Why should we come back to your firing squad?'

'I admire your spirit,' Swayne said, 'and it was decent of you to warn the men. You have my oath as an officer that if you return peacefully, at once, you will simply be held in brig and receive a fair trial when the lawful government has been restored.'

His voice was fading as the distance lengthened. The stars crackled their scorn through every word. But the ring and cold in that tone remained clear:

'If you do not come back, if you get away, I shall maintain the *Vega* on alert for the week or so which is the maximum time you could possibly survive. However, that will tie up too much manpower; the armament project will be halted. I don't want that, nor do I want to take the risk, even if it is small, that you have a cache somewhere, on some orbiting rock, that I don't know about. Therefore, if you do not reverse acceleration at once, I shall fire a missile.'

Fraser stared at Lorraine. She shook her head, eyes blind with tears.

'Stop playing hero,' Swayne urged. 'Your death won't gain anything for your cause. Come back, and you may yet have a chance to be of service.'

He spoke almost at the limit of audibility now, a ghost's whisper. 'All right,' Fraser croaked, 'you win. Roger and out.'

He snapped off the transmitter. Lorraine's gauntleted fists beat the arms of her chair. 'I'd rather be dead,' she wept.

'You may get your wish,' he said harshly. 'I agreed just to gain us some time. The longer the wait before he shoots that missile, the more distance it'll have to cover, and the larger the volume of space in which it'll have to hunt around for us.'

'You mean –' She stiffened. 'We might evade it ... altogether?'

'N-no, I'm afraid not. We haven't got that much of a head start.' He reached for the main switch, but withdrew his hand. 'Uh-uh. We'd better stay at low thrust. If they detected a jetblast with a red shift, they'd fire immediately, and the missile's detectors would latch onto us for keeps. As is – Lory, this is a long chance to take, and even if it succeeds, I don't know how to reach Blocksberg. Tell me if I have a right to.' He sighed. 'People depend on me. And then there's you, you've got your life ahead of you.'

'How much would that be worth, after they put me through "re-education"? But Eve and your kids –'

'Hell! We'll try it! Our own radar will tell us when the missile's found us and started homing in. Then we'll open our engine up. Full acceleration. This boat's got more thrust than we can maybe stand, not having any booster drugs along, but we'll try.'

She had stopped crying. The tears still glistened on her face, but she watched him unwaveringly and her tone held only puzzlement: 'I don't get it. I thought you intended to play hide-and-seek, hoping the missile wouldn't spot us before it ran out of fuel. But if you don't think that's possible how can you ever believe we can outrace it?'

'We can't, over the long haul. But if the race is short enough perhaps –' unconsciously, his hand closed over hers and squeezed – 'perhaps we can get to safety ahead of it.'

'Where?'

He pointed to the starboard front viewscreen. Jupiter filled its darkness.

148

17

As they came up the gorge that cut through the north side of the Wilderwall, they heard the first drums. Theor stopped in his tracks. The army behind rattled slowly to a halt. Like a single animal it strained to hear; but by then the beats had ceased.

For a space Theor stood in a silence broken only by the whine of wind above the cliffs. They hemmed him in on either side, blackly outlined against a strip of sky almost as dark with clouds and evening. Trees grew sparsely on top. Their limbs writhed in the cold sliding of the air. Down here on the bottom of the ravine, shadows were thick and the host was a vague mass, faintly glowing by its infrared radiation, the chillier weapons and armour revealed in silhouette. The detritus that carpeted the way was sharp under his feet.

'Did you hear that?' he asked. 'Yes,' Walfilo said. 'Watchers' signals.'

The drums muttered again, somewhere on the heights to the left.

'This is an ill place to be caught,' said Walfilo. 'They could hurl stones at us from above.'

Theor debated whether to advance or retreat. The entrance of the gorge was closer than the pass ahead. By going back, he would soon reach ground where his soldiers could deploy. But then they might sit for days awaiting attack, while Leenant and Pors starved in Nyarr. 'We'll proceed forward,' he said.

'I would not ordinarily counsel that,' Walfilo muttered,

149

'but our mission is so forlorn anyway –' He clapped his hands together. An adjutant hurried up. 'Dispatch a patrol to find out whatever it can about that messenger. Have the rest close ranks and continue.'

The army's own drums banged forth the order. Echoes rolled emptily from wall to wall. Ice alloy clanked, stones clattered, feet shuffled in their thousands, and the Nyarrans moved on.

The murk deepened as night fell, but there was no stopping. One couldn't lose his way here! The scouts returned with the expected report: no trace of a spy. He had all the mountains to hide in when they approached. However, more encouragingly, there was no indication of a barbarian warband either.

Or was that anything to cheer about? Theor felt his mouth tighten as grimly as Walfilo's.

They reached Windgate Pass near midnight. The cliffs dropped away behind them and a rough but open slope lay ahead, downward to their own country. Theor could see a remote gleam, the luminous Brantor winding south toward Nyarr and the ocean. Even after he had gotten camp established, he slept little.

Sometime before dawn, the drumming roused him. He started out of uneasy dreams, momentarily looking for lightning and rain. But no, it was another signal, off in the night – and not a short-range one this time. Those thunderpulses could only come from one of the biggest military drums, of the sort that needed four Jovians to carry it but in this atmosphere could be heard for ten miles or more.

Others had been wakened too. He heard cries in the dark, overridden by the rolling, crashing blows off the heights. Then Walfilo's command bit through the racket. His own drummers repeated it: *Silence, silence, silence.* The strokes above ended almost simultaneously, and a thrumming hush arose.

150

Abruptly Theor realised what his general had in mind. He turned his head south, held every muscle moveless, and listened. It came soon, dwarfed almost to nothing by that immense night, but every note clear. *Boom-bom-brrr-bom! Boom-bom-brrr-bom! Ra-ta-ta-bom-boom, ra-ta-ta-bom-boom, brrr-ta, brrr-ta, bom-bom, bom-bom . . .*

Walfilo issued another series of orders. Feet thudded and weapons clinked. Theor followed the noise, arriving just as a good-sized patrol galloped off. Close at hand, Walfilo's skin radiated brighter than normal, so that Theor could make out the wrinkles which scored the face. 'I sent them off in the hope of catching those spies,' the older male said.

'I realise as much. But may they not be ambushed?'

'No, the enemy scouts must be very few. A larger party would be heard by us whenever they approached near enough to observe anything useful.'

'They must be Ulunt-Khazul,' Theor said dully.

Walfilo spat. 'What else? Chalkhiz knows more local geography than even I feared he would. Almost at once after the last battle, he must have established pickets to watch every route by which we might return, and lines of communication from them to his headquarters. There is no more chance of surprising him. Every move we make will be known.'

Theor slumped. 'What should we do?'

'We could withdraw.'

'No.'

'We could establish ourselves here, then. It's a highly defensible position.'

'What use would that be? He would simply take Nyarr, and afterward deal with us at his leisure.'

'True. I see only one course, then – to proceed openly. Not stop to make rafts, just march as fast as we can, feeding ourselves at the ranches along the way. But first we should make some rough fortifications here, so that we have

151

a strong point to retreat to if we are beaten in the field.'

'You mean when we are beaten, do you not?' Theor agreed unwillingly. The delay would give time to the enemy, but he knew too well the weakness of his forces.

Dawn broke in fiery clouds and nacreous mist on the plain. The army fell to work, dragging stones into place for a series of walls across the pass, heaping other boulders up to roll down on attackers. Theor lost himself in toil. But from time to time he heard the drums talking in the distance. It was small consolation that the patrol had captured the one on this ridge. The operators had gotten clean away.

The planet spun through another night before Walfilo conceded that preparations were as adequate as possible. The next morning the army came down the Wilderwall. It took them the whole day to reach the foothills. They camped by the Brantor. Toward sunrise Theor heard drums again, nearer than could be accounted for by his own advance.

They started off at an early hour. Their food supplies were nearly exhausted, hunters could bring in only a niggard ration, and the flat pasturelands were still a couple of days off. The Nyarrans plodded thin and mute along the river-bank, over the rolling, sparsely wooded landscape. The current ran louder than their footfalls, white-streaked on its way to the sea.

We will be in better shape when we can commandeer from the ranches, Theor assured himself.

Late in the day, a forgar landed. The rider sprang off and raced to the head of the army. 'Reeve – General – I've seen the enemy. His entire host, I think.'

'What?' Walfilo bellowed. 'So soon? Impossible!'

'They're in ships. The Brantor is covered with their ships.' As if it had heard, a drum started up, miles away but strong and arrogant.

'Pulled by their beasts?' Theor gripped his axe helve till

his knuckles creaked. 'Yes, they could come that fast, even upstream. But are you certain of their numbers?'

'I counted from above. More than two sixty-fours of craft, each loaded with warriors.'

'But then they must have raised the siege of Nyarr.'

Walfilo snorted. 'Not exactly. They've withdrawn from its neighbourhood, but I hardly think the people inside can venture far out. For if they do, the returning Ulunt-Khazul might well fall on them unawares.'

'The defenders could sally, to attack the enemy rear.'

'How? Those ships outpace any land army. No, Chalkhiz has seen an opportunity to defeat us in detail.' Walfilo rubbed his massive chin. 'Of course, if there is a sally, and it caught up with him while he is still engaging us –' He glowered at the earth for a while, then said:

'It's our only hope. We must fly the message to Nyarr, that they are to hazard everything – though little there is to lose – and hurry north. Meanwhile we must prolong the battle, retreating back to Windgate Pass. Perhaps Chalkhiz will not realise our strategy in time.' The soldier shook his head. 'Of course, even if it works for us, I doubt we can prevail. So many will have fallen by the time the reinforcements come, that the Ulunt-Khazul can likely handle what's left without overmuch trouble. Still, it will raise the price they pay for our country.'

Theor mastered a sickness and asked, 'When will they fall on us?'

'Ush. I daresay they'll camp tonight, lest unseen rocks tear the bottom out of the ships. Tomorrow morning. Short time to make ready.'

He summoned his underlings and began giving commands. *I wish I could lose myself thus,* Theor thought.

The Nyarrans moved onto a hill some distance from the river. Its saddle-shaped ridge would protect their flanks, and the swale behind offered a northward line of retreat. The bushes were soon trampled into mud, and the slopes became strewn with red centaur bodies, sharpening weapons, talking in a desultory way, staring into the sky or past the woods to the hazed mountains. Theor could count the ribs on them. There was no protest when Walfilo ordered most of the forgars slaughtered for meat. Too few were left to be of much service in battle, and an unfed army wouldn't last a day. Nonetheless Theor had trouble getting the food down.

I brought us to this, he thought bitterly. He almost looked forward to the spear thrust that would end his guilt.

The sunlight disappeared in the west. Not many Nyarrans slept well. Theor heard stirrings the whole night as he stood wakeful.

In the morning, a shadow passed through the fog and landed on the hillcrest, an aerial observer using one of the half-dozen animals which had been spared. He reported that the Ulunt-Khazul had grounded their ships, tethered their swimming beasts to them, and set off afoot. They seemed to know just where their opponents were. Well, they were swimmers themselves; a scout, gliding along with little more than his eyes above the river surface, could have gone ahead of his own people.

The mist lifted. Ice shimmered in the Nyarran ranks. Three tattered banners fluttered listlessly over the taut, massed faces, scale-armoured bodies, and stubbornly planted feet. Theor stood near the middle of the front line, with Walfilo on his left. They could think of nothing to say to each other. It seemed long before the Ulunt-Khazul emerged from the woods at the river bank.

They formed for the charge under the volcanic rumble of their drums, line after line of great grey thick-tailed shapes, fangs gleaming under the overshadowing helmets, menace painted on shields and cuirasses and flags. *Nearly thrice our number*, Theor estimated. But that no longer seemed important. There was only the day's work to do. He took a firmer grip on his own shield and swung his axe.

154

'See there!' Walfilo pointed. 'The chiefly banner.'

'Hurgh?'

'I paid heed to such details on Gillen Beach. Chalkhiz himself is here today.'

The drums by the river broke into a steady tattoo. Footfalls answered them, a *pad-pad-pad* which became a sound like surf as the enemy neared. Voices rose curtly from the Nyarran lines, and the spears of the second and third ranks snapped down past the shoulders of the first. The Ulunt-Khazul couched their own lances and broke into a gallop.

Closer, closer, closer. The few forgars swooped, the riders dropped stones, but to no effect that Theor could see. He remembered, briefly and distantly, his experiments with a bow and arrow, carried out at Fraser's suggestion. It hadn't been practical under Jovian conditions. Would that it had. His gaze focused on a hostile warrior who would evidently be the first one to come against him. The fellow had a partly healed wound on his left cheek. *Let's give it a mate.* Theor raised his axe.

With a roar and a kettle clang, the Ulunt-Khazul fell upon the Nyarran spears. Their shields and horn breast-plates protected most from being spitted, but the momentum of their charge was spent. Theor saw one spear-shaft snapped by the collision of a giant on his right. The Ulunt-Khazuli stumbled. Another spear flicked out and caught him in the unarmoured abdomen. He shouted – it could not be heard through the din – and struck back with a saw-toothed club.

Then Theor's antagonist was upon him, shoving the pikes aside and stabbing with his lance at the Reeve. Theor caught the thrust on his shield. It glided off. His axe crashed down. It struck a shoulderpiece. The warrior growled and jabbed at Theor's throat. Theor beat the shaft aside. A powerful hand shot out and caught his weapon-wielding wrist. He raised his shield and chopped the edge onto that arm. The Ulunt-Khazuli let go. Theor smote him twice on the helmet. He staggered. Theor took the one step forward permitted a soldier in the line and struck across the enemy warrior's back. The impact shivered along his own sinews. The grey barrel of the body crumpled. Blood ran gaudy. The Ulunt-Khazuli sank to earth, still alive. The one behind trampled over him to get at Theor.

The Nyarrans had held firm, the charge had failed, now it was mass opposed to mass. The rear lines on either side thrust, sliced, clubbed with their spears. The first ranks stabbed and smote. Theor slipped in blood. That was fortunate for him; a knife whirred where he had been. He raised his forequarters and struck sideways at a leg. He didn't know what damage was done, for the tide of combat took that warrior from sight. He rose to confront another. They traded blows, axe on shield, and Theor felt his lesser strength melting under the shocks.

What was that vibration beneath his mailcoat?

An impact banged nearly hard enough to break his arm. He chopped wildly, missed – the Ulunt-Khazuli grinned and pressed inward. Theor was only half aware of his danger. He could not hear with his ribs, but he could feel – the communicator on his breast had come alive.

He warded off another blow, but sank purposely beneath it. The webbed feet of his enemy ramped across him. *Let the male behind me take over. This is more important.* Theor held the shield above him and squirmed between the churning legs.

Or does it matter? I have no right to desert. He glimpsed Walfilo, painted with blood, hewing and hewing. *I left his side when he needed me.* Now Theor was past the front line, in among his own spearfolk. He ignored their aghast stares as he rose and pushed through to the rear. But he could not drive away the image of Walfilo.

18

After five gravities of deceleration, the change to free fall was like stepping off a precipice edge. Fraser's brain whirled into red-streaked night.

A thread of consciousness remained, quivering with pain. The fear of death drove him to climb it, hand over hand, again and again slipping back into a gulf that tolled. When finally he broke through and remembered who he was, he felt a weak astonishment that only minutes had passed.

Perhaps that was too long. He couldn't see the missile yet, among the stars which frosted the forward viewscreens; but the radar said it would soon close with him. In a convulsive movement, he activated the steering nozzles. The *Olympia* spun about and faced into Jupiter.

There was no longer a planet to be seen against space, he was too close, there was only a monstrous vision of clouds, yellow and brown and cobbled with shadows. A storm marched behind that curtain, a cauldron of lightning ten thousand miles wide. The horizon tilted into sight. He stopped the ship's rotation and threw the main switch. Once more his own weight suffocated him, his gear and body throbbed in time with the jets.

High thrust to make the crossing as quick as possible had had to be countered by equally stiff deceleration, lest the hull disintegrate in the Jovian atmosphere. The enemy rocket was under no such necessity. It was fast overhauling its prey.

Fraser stole a glance at Lorraine. She had passed out more than an hour ago. Her face was smeared with blood from the nose, and he couldn't tell if she still breathed. *Well, she won't feel what's to come, anyhow. Maybe I won't either. We could crack open when we strike, if the missile doesn't get us first.* He knew he should be thinking of Eve at this penultimate moment, but there was too much to do, bringing the ship in at what he could only hope was the correct angle. And he was too weary, too beaten and bruised by the passage.

Here we go!

He looked behind. A thin silvery streak swelled in the after screen.

Then a troll's fist slammed into him, the universe exploded, and he watched no longer.

So steep is the density gradient of Jupiter's gaseous envelope that there was little heating while the *Olympia* flashed down through the uppermost layers – only enough to turn the hull red on the outside. A second or two afterward, she struck a level which, under her speed, acted as a solid, elastic surface. In huge, shaken bounds, like a stone skipped across a lake she rounded the curve of the world. The missile's hunter-pilot circuits were not intelligent enough to foresee that and change course while there was still time. It screamed straight down, an artificial meteorite. Ablation peeled away its skin. The chemical warhead exploded. The Jovian night did not notice that short, feeble burst of light, and a thunderclap drowned the noise.

Rapidly losing velocity, the *Olympia* spiralled toward the surface. The cherry glare of her exterior vanished in stratospheric cold. Great winds buffeted her to and fro, back and forth, and filled her full of their shrieks. That roused Fraser. He struggled back toward awareness, remembered that he must get clear before the final plunge began, and unleashed the jets. Time dragged toward eternity while he beat his way starward. He knew only pain. His bleared eyes needed a while to recognise the sight of open

158

space. *Now ... get her into orbit ... stay awake till you've established orbit, you've got to, you've got to ... you have –* He let go all holds and drew the dear oblivion about him.

The first thing he observed on waking was the clock. A dozen hours were gone. He blinked around the cabin. Free fall embraced his aching body, Jupiter glowed warm amber in the port and forward screens, the ship brimmed with an unbelievable stillness. Lorraine floated toward him. He saw that she had cleaned herself up and looked almost rested.

'How are you, Mark?' she asked softly.

He shook arms and legs, twisted his neck, inhaled and exhaled. 'Ugh! Uh, I – I don't think anything's busted. You?'

'Same. I came to a while back. I wondered whether to do anything for you or not – oh, God, I was worried! – but you seemed better off sleeping.' She stopped her flight with a hand on his shoulder. 'Now I'm going to spend a few minutes simply enjoying the miracle, that we both came through.'

They exchanged a long-lived smile. She belied her words by offering him stimulant and analgesic from the scanty kit they had carried with them. He shoved the pills through the eating valve on his helmet, followed by a long suck of water from the suit's bottle. Well-being coursed through every cell. 'How about some chow?' he said.

'I haven't touched any myself.' Her happiness disappeared. 'We've only got those few standard food bars.'

'And need some now. We've a lot of recuperation to do, girl.'

Afterward Fraser followed her example and entered one of the emergency boxes for a wash. It wasn't much bigger than a coffin, and a man with no other recourse could do little except lie there, breathing the few hours' worth of air in its attached bottle and hoping for rescue. Squirming, Fraser swabbed himself off with alcohol tapped from the inopera-

159

tive water cycler, and did what little he could to clean the space outfit crowded and collapsed in the box with him. The stubble on his face must perforce remain there. But it felt so good to get the crusted blood and sweat off that he could tolerate residual discomforts with ease.

Returning forward, he found Lorraine with eyes on the planet. She glanced at him and back. Her voice whispered in his earplugs: 'I never knew anything could be so terrible and so beautiful.'

He nodded. 'It compensates for a lot, that view.'

She turned away and said with quick desperation, 'Not for our failure, though. We have failed, haven't we?'

'Don't say that,' he chided her, well aware that he was whistling past a graveyard. 'We outran and outfoxed a space missile, probably the first time an unarmed ship ever has. We're free.'

'Free to die of thirst, unless our air gives out beforehand. We can't even leave the Jovian System with any hope of success.' She smote the bulkhead with her fist, and rebounded. 'If we just had navigational equipment, we could still win, you know. We could put the ship on course for Earth, write our message, and deliver it dead. Isn't there some way you could improvise – ?'

'No. I don't know whether to be sorry or not, but even given instruments and data, we couldn't use them to any effect. To arrive in time, we have to travel a hyperbolic velocity. Since the *Olympia* was never intended to do that, she hasn't got an autopilot which could make rendezvous at the end of such an orbit without human assistance.'

'If Jupiter were only the least bit like Earth!'

An oath broke from Fraser.

'What's the trouble?' she asked.

'No trouble. I got a sudden idea. Crazy wild, but – ' He pondered. 'What we need besides pilot stuff is air and water; we can go without food for the transit time. Well, Jupiter has them.'

160

'What?'

'We've a big cargo space. There's ice down on the surface. Theor's people can load it aboard for us. I should be able to rig a gadget for electrolysing oxygen from some of the water. We have a pretty well-equipped workshop along.'

'But the methane, ammonia, all the poisons. We can't get them out of the mixture . . . can we?'

'I don't know. It doesn't seem plausible. Still – And I ought to call Theor anyway.' Fraser settled in the pilot chair and plugged in a radio jack.

The ship carried a small neutrino set, too weak for any but short-range communication. In orbit, though, he could employ the relay satellites. He hadn't the data tables by which to send a beam, but he must be close enough for a broadcast to reach the nearest one. He adjusted the dials. 'Theor,' he called. 'Mark speaking. Are you there?'

'That's a weird language,' Lorraine said. After a while: 'No answer, eh?'

Fraser sighed. 'None. I'll try the frequencies used by the other personal transceivers, but I'm afraid none will reply. His cause lost out also.' He turned his face away from the planet, but even after they should have adapted, his eyes were too full of tears to see the stars.

'Well –'

'Marhk! Kstorho g'ng korach!'

'Him! – I wish I had a God to thank.' Fraser sagged where he floated. 'How are you, boy?'

'Sore beset, mind-brother. I have crept away from what may be our last combat. But gladness can yet touch me that you live.'

'Tell me. I'm not far off, as you can guess from the absence of transmission lag. Maybe, even – But tell.'

Fraser heard out the story. Numb with dismay, he recounted his own situation.

'Strange how our lives intertwine,' Theor mused. 'I know

161

not what counsel to give you. As for myself, I must return to the fight. I sit on the ridge above and see my folk die under the axes. Yet we strove well, you and I. Did we not?'

'If I could help – Wait!' Fraser yelled. 'I can!'

'Hurgh? Locked in your vessel as you must be?'

'Look, Theor. I don't want to waste time in arguments. I'm coming down. Stay put. Keep yourself out of combat. I'll need your help to find you. Can you hold out a few hours yet?'

'Yes ... yes, surely. I expect the enemy will soon withdraw, to rest a while ere charging again. We had hopes of playing him for days, a running off-and-on battle – But Mark, you cannot, ill prepared as you are.'

'Stay put, I told you. Wait for my next call. I'm coming!'

Fraser snapped off the radio, which would be useless during atmospheric flight, and turned to Lorraine. 'Strap in, girl. I'm sorry to do this to you, but we survived five gees, so I guess we can stand half that value for a bit.'

She made no demurral, went quietly to her chair and got to work in the harness. As he fastened himself in place, Fraser explained how matters stood.

'At least we'll win his war for him,' he finished.

She reached over to touch him. 'That's very like you, Mark.'

'Besides ... there's an idea at the back of my mind, something I can't quite pin down, that might work better for us than – Well, I'm going to bleed some bathyscaphe gas into the main compartment. A few atmospheres' worth. The descent wasn't originally planned to be that way, but there is provision for doing it as an emergency measure, and I don't fancy sitting in vacuum with Jovian air pressure outside.'

The gas rushed in with a hollow noise, the quality of light and shadow changed as dust particles became airborne, the awakening engine boomed through ears as well as flesh.

Jetfire blossomed aft. The *Olympia* spiralled backward and down. That was a slow descent, with twenty-six miles per second of orbital velocity to shed, but neither Fraser nor Lorraine spoke much during it. The sight that grew before them, and finally engulfed them, was too overpowering.

The stars vanished. The sky turned from black to deep violet, where high ice-clouds coruscated in sunlight. Below lay the banded ocean of air, a thousand hues tumbled and streaming, with sheets of lightning at play between them.

When the instruments showed air density equivalent to Earth's at twenty miles – here, the altitude was much less – Fraser cut the space drive and went over to the aerodynamic system. The uppermost stratum of ammonia clouds was immediately beneath him. He entered it.

Blackness closed in, above, around, below. He switched the screens to infrared conversion, reducing the wavelengths that penetrated this far, or were produced thermally, to ones that he could see. But little appeared except blue-green whirls. He advanced cautiously. The time grew long that he spent in formlessness. The ship clove atmosphere with an ever deeper sound that seemed at last to permeate his whole being, take him up into itself so that he rode in a Nirvana of thunder.

An electric discharge flashed white, lighting up cliffs and canyons of cloud for mile after vertical mile, each bank the size of a terrestrial continent. The noise and the gust that followed made the ship lunge like a rowelled horse. Instruments danced crazily. Fraser's body slammed against his harness with the whole brutal weight of four hundred and twenty pounds that now burdened him. Each movement was an effort. His touch on the controls made the console ring. But he was too absorbed in grandeur to pay heed.

The turbulence fell behind; once more the *Olympia* droned through an abyssal calm. In one sense, it was illusory, for the pressure at this level would have crumpled any other ship men had ever built. And still it rose as she descended.

But she was meant for this place. Cabin and engine room were burrows in an ovoid block of alloy steel whose near-perfect crystals locked each molecule with a force close to the ultimate. Only the airlock and the cargo compartment doors broke that surface, and they were equally massive, squeezed ever more tightly shut by the outside atmosphere. There were no ports to be shattered. Instruments and viewscreens employed solid-state devices akin to those which had been landed on Jupiter. As far as sheer strength was concerned this part of the *Olympia* could have gone a ways below the solar photosphere.

About a fourth of the hold was similarly constructed, in order to bring back minerals whose allotropy required Jovian surface conditions. The rest, though sturdier than spaceship hulls to be found anywhere else, amounted only to a number of cells which would take samples of atmosphere at various higher altitudes. At the moment, they were all open and had no net force on them.

Engine energy had been shunted from the rockets to a set of turbojets. And above, a flexible, immensely tough bag had expanded. Controlled by a barometer, pumps filled it with gas supplied by the breakdown of carbohydrate; heat flowed in to keep the interior less dense than the cold native hydrogen-helium which surrounded it at equal pressure. Thus the overall effective weight of the system was almost nil.

The *Olympia* was, in effect, a space-going bathyscaphe. She did not so much fly as swim through the Jovian sky.

Almost like old times, in the seas of Earth, Fraser dreamed. Then again the hull rocked and yawed, a wolf howl ripped at him, he heard the clang of ammonia hailstones and felt the metal shudder beneath their blows. Lorraine's cry came tiny: 'They must be as massive as I am! What if they tear the bag open?'

'Then we're done for,' he said between his teeth, and fought the controls.

By halting the gas pumps, lowering the nose, and pouring on power, he broke through the bottom of the storm. It didn't reach the ground against the pressure from below; it couldn't! When once again they were in a green calm, Fraser needed several minutes to stop shaking.

His god-sense was gone. He felt very mortal. But suddenly he entered into wonder.

The surface became visible.

No little distorted glimpses through a screen, no clumsy Jovian attempt at description, had prepared him for this. Overhead arched a golden heaven, where the lowest clouds floated turquoise, ultramarine and copper. Rain rushed from one bank on the northern horizon, a cataract to dwarf Niagara, silver-glinting, with lightning in the smoke-blue caverns above. Dusk lingered over an ocean in the west; and under it, each wave shone, spouting sparks. Rollers more huge and rapid than a tidal wave at home marched east into daylight, shining like damascened steel, burst on the shore and flung foam so high that it made a continuous glitter in the air. Beyond, a plain stretched boundless, blue and yellow bushes, a forest whose branches rippled in the wind and shook forth eerily shaped clusters of leaves, until the eastern edge of the world lost itself in gold-bronze vapours. A low escarpment rose in the south, blackly and metallically agleam, ice cliffs down which a river leaped foaming toward the sea.

Stunned into muteness, Fraser and Lorraine hu..g there and looked, lost themselves in the scene, for a time beyond time. Nothing but the memory of Theor roused the man.

Reluctantly, he studied his instruments. The powerful automatic radio beacon that had been landed close to Nyarr in anticipation of the human visit registered faintly. So his

165

dead reckoning as he came down hadn't been too far off. He reduced altitude and drove the ship northward.

'Look yonder,' Lorraine pointed. A flock of devilfish shapes winged half a mile away. They shone as if burnished. Down on the plain, a herd of six-legged animals with magnificent horns bolted when the *Olympia* passed over. There were thousands of them; the earthquake roll of their feet reached so high that it was picked up by the sonic relays.

'And I always thought Jupiter was ... was a kind of frozen hell,' she faltered.

'To the Jovians, Earth is a kind of hot hell,' he replied.

'But, I mean, well, this splendour! This much life!'

He nodded his heavy head. 'Uh-huh. That's the real wonder of the universe, I suppose. Life.'

Her bitterness returned. 'And we have such a short time alive, and still people spoil it.'

'Jovians do too. They aren't so very unlike us, eh?'

'Your friend Theor,' she said uncertainly. 'He's got a family, didn't you tell me?'

'Yes. He's quite devoted to them.'

'Lucky fellow.'

He gave her a startled glance, but she had averted her face.

Presently he spied a river that must be the Brantor. He followed it until the radio compass said he was above Nyarr, and hovered for a look. There was plainly an extensive artificial area below, though it resembled more a cultivated maze than any city he had imagined. Through high magnification, he saw crowds scurry about, staring and gesturing at him.

He activated the neutrino set. 'Theor, are you still okay? How goes the fight?'

'Worse for us than we hoped. Nigh that I despaired of you, Mark. They have not yet driven us off the hilltop, but each attack they make thins our lines. Where are you?'

'At your home town.'

'Lives the city yet?'

'Yes. No one's camped outside, either. But they haven't tried to contact me.'

'Give them time, the councillors who know how to use the equipment. You must be a fearful apparition.'

'We can't wait for them, you and I. Now describe your location exactly, and your people, so I won't attack the wrong army. Then get your commander to start his retreat during the next lull in the fighting, over the hill to the other side.'

Fraser stopped. Only now did the implications of his tactics become clear to him. He shrank from them. 'Hold on!' he said waveringly. 'Can you communicate with the enemy?'

'I believe Chalkhiz, their leader, understands our drum code as well as our language.'

'Warn him that the oracle is coming, and will destroy him if he doesn't surrender.'

'How he will laugh!'

'No doubt. But still, with some advance notice, they may suffer fewer casualties.'

'You do not know what they have done to us, Mark, or you would have no care for them.'

'I like to think that I would.'

'For your sake, then, it shall be done. Now, as to the information you need —' Fraser had known Theor long enough to recognise the joy behind those few crisp words. It heartened him a little.

'Check,' he said. 'One more thing. Warn your own people not to look at me after I arrive. They're to cover their faces, and crawl behind their shields if possible. Got it? I'm on my way.'

The *Olympia* surged forward. Lorraine regarded Fraser

long. 'Isn't your idea working out?' she asked. 'You look like death.'

'Oh, it is,' he bit off. 'That's what's wrong.'

The time was all too short before he passed over the ships and sea monsters of Ulunt-Khazul. Beyond, the forest opened on undulant country with another ice range in the north. It seethed with Jovians. Fraser's untrained eye could make little sense of the ordering and movement, but he saw that a lesser group were bunched on one slope of a hill while a larger one was advancing from the river side. The crest between was littered with dead; they looked as empty and pathetic as any slain man.

'Theor, are you ready?'

'Aye!'

Fraser snapped his teeth together and brought the ship down.

He had cherished a hope that the invaders would flee at the sight of him. But they had too much discipline, too much bravery. The sonics brought him a challenge cry, an eruption of drumbeats and clang of weapons. He saw a ripple go through their mass, they locked ranks and raised their lances in defiance of every god this land might loose on them.

'Theor, I see an extra-large flag at the point of their wedge formation. Is that where their chief would be?'

'Indeed so. Chalkhiz fights in his own van. I feel ashamed that I did not likewise.'

'You and me both. Well – I'll go after Chalkhiz.'

The ship tilted around until her stern jets pointed at the prideful banner. Fraser gunned the rockets.

It was a low thrust, barely sufficing to push reaction mass out against the atmosphere. But the energy required for that much was so great that only the riven atom could yield it. And the gas emerged at thousands of degrees.

To Jovian senses, the world lit up as if all the lightnings

that ever raged had struck in this one place. The sky turned molten, the earth glowed, rocks melted and ran over ground that exploded in live ammonia steam. Air flamed with momentary incandescence, wrapped itself around each living thing and consumed the flesh. Then the shock wave came. The ground heaved up, a wave that ran out and out until it struck the rise and brought the hillside down in avalanche. Dust and smoke whirled in a cloud, through which dreadful fragments went flying. The roar which followed seemed to burst heads open. Back and forth the echoes beat, shock upon shock, and as they faded a great brief wind whistled across desolation.

Fraser did not know how many Ulunt-Khazul perished in that circle of Ragnarok. He dared not reckon them up. Still less dared he look on that which crawled about at the edges, blind and charred, and screamed. He could only remind himself, over and over and over, that thousands didn't appear to be seriously hurt, that they galloped in every direction, their weapons cast away, their will utterly broken, crazy with panic, no longer a conquering army, no longer anything.

'Mark, mind-brother, deliverer,' Theor chanted. The drums of Nyarr crashed triumph behind him.

'Did your people come through unharmed?' Fraser asked mechanically.

'Ush, yes, we were well protected. Already Walfilo issues commands for detachments to go capture the enemy ships and as many warriors as possible. Not that they are ever likely to rally, but they could turn bandit if we le' them escape. Herded off to Rollarik, they will be less troublesome . . . Can you land? The first man on this world!'

'Sure, I can land,' said Fraser, and wept.

Lorraine unstrapped herself, dragged her weighted body to his side, and cradled his head in its helmet against her armoured breast. 'Oh Mark, darling, don't let it hurt you.

Think how many more lives would have been lost if you hadn't come and, and saved a whole civilization. Think what we've got left to do at home. You have to free us, too, Mark.'

He tore loose from her; she saw the upsurge in him and he shouted: 'We can, by glory!'

19

He was less certain – he had no certainty whatsoever – by the time they were ready to go. The long confinement in his spacesuit was driving his body toward revolt; it sent him petitions of itch, manifestos of stench and impeachments of nausea. Matters might paradoxically have been less endurable were he not so worn down by hunger and gravity. At least that enabled him to spend most of the hours asleep while Theor's people loaded his ship.

Now he sat erect in the pilot chair, Lorraine beside him, and wondered how he had ever imagined so fantastic a scheme as his might work. Though there was no alternative, was there? They could refine water for him in the firepots of Ath, but Theor doubted that the smith community, disrupted by the war, would be able to resume operations soon enough to do the humans any good. Maybe, given a rested and nourished brain, Fraser could have thought of some less precarious plan. But the heavy blood was unwilling to rise in him, his ankles swelled and his head felt scooped-out, empty. Jupiter was no place for any man to linger long; and if the man had spent the last dozen years on Ganymede, and was getting old . . .

He stared out at a wild and marvellous sunset. The disc itself was not visible through the many cloud strata overhead, but a part of the sky was always brighter than the rest. That luminosity had slipped behind the western mists and turned them to fire. The light reached the northern scarp and flared back off it, as if the Wilderwall had become molten and yet somehow remained standing. Trees shook their branches aloft in a slow wind, which blew with a sound like the ocean. Fog had begun to rise on the open country, a purple gloaming over the land; but the river still gleamed sword bright.

'I wish –'

'What, Mark?'

'Foolishness. That I could come back here some day.'

'Why not? With booster drugs and proper equipment, you could spend several Earth-days at a time. Don't you think I want to return? But I'm a woman, and untrained for the work, and ... I never will. You, though, with your knowledge, and with everyone so grateful to you – why, the next expedition will insist on taking you.'

' 'Fraid not. Any service I could do, could just as well be done from an orbital post. I've no business coming down here. Pharmacopoeia or not, I can't stand the gaff as well or as long as a younger man; I'd hinder the work. So, well, we'll have an unfulfilled wish in common, Lory. Along with everything else.'

She bit her lip and made no reply.

'I do wish, however, I weren't so tired and lightheaded,' Fraser said. 'I can't appreciate what's out there. It doesn't quite register. You're in better shape. Look close for me, will you, Lory? And listen to the wind and feel the weight, even. So you can tell me afterward what it was like.'

'If there is an afterward,' she said.

'We have to assume we'll carry off the plan, or what is there for us?'

'I wasn't thinking about the operation against Swayne, Mark. I meant after that.'

Theor called out an order. The Jovians who had been at work by the cargo hatch dispersed. It hadn't been fair to make them load the high-pressure compartment with rock, almost immediately after their battle. Fraser could see how the round heads were bowed, crests drooping, arms hanging

172

loose, sturdy striped bodies barely able to shuffle away toward the river. But they could rest now before starting home. The humans' work was hardly begun.

Theor himself came around to the bow. The sunset light gleamed off the disc on his breast and the big eyes. 'We are done, mind-brother,' he said. 'Would that we could do more. But we have nothing left to offer you except our hopes.'

'You've done plenty,' Fraser said.

'Must you go at once?'

'Yes.'

'I have not even seen you, behind that hull. And our hands will never clasp. Ush-heu, this is a strange universe.'

'I'll call you when I'm able.'

'I shall have no ease until you do. May the Powers ride with you always.'

'Goodbye, Theor.'

'Farewell, Mark.'

The Jovian moved off to a safe distance. Fraser worked the controls to close the hatch and start the engine. Heat expanded the gas bag. The ship rose. Theor stood waving. Fraser and Lorraine watched him until he vanished in distance and night.

The passage up was slow. Fraser had to bleed the bag, lest pressure rip it open. At appropriate heights he closed off the air sample cells. The ship moved sluggishly, weighted by her cargo. He dreaded a storm. But none was encountered. It was as if the whole planet wanted to aid him.

In the end he glimpsed the sun, started the jets, and felt his heart labour under acceleration. When finally he judged they were in orbit, the simple act of turning off the thrust was almost as much as he could do. Sleep smote him where he sat.

He awoke hours afterward, weak, sore and ravenous, but more refreshed than he had expected. His mind was almost unnaturally clear. Yet the time on Jupiter did not seem quite real, it was like something he had dreamed long ago. Nothing existed but the cabin, the woman, and the task.

'I think we'd better eat our last food bars, don't you?' Lorraine said. 'We'll need our strength.'

'Uh-huh. Break 'em out, will you?'

The stuff was tasteless in his mouth. He drank deep; there was no longer any reason to hoard water. 'Well,' he said, 'now we have to figure out our switching arrangement.'

'I've already done that,' Lorraine answered. 'I came to well before you did,' She pointed at a tangle of tools, wire, and replacement-parts metal, netted in place on one of the bunks. 'In fact, I've almost got it finished.'

'Good girl.' Fraser regarded her for a space that grew. The amber light from the planet was gentle to her features, toning down their strength, lending a glamour of which he was much too aware. 'You know,' he said, almost involuntarily, 'you're a beautiful girl.'

'Don't Mark,' she murmured; and then: 'No, do. For this one time. There can't be another. Can there?'

'I guess not.'

'I'm going back to Earth,' she said.

'No!'

'I have to. It's the only way out.'

'Well . . . I wish you wouldn't,' he said.

'No, you don't wish that, Mark. Not down inside.'

'I could envy the man who marries you.'

'I do envy your wife. But you know, I'm not jealous of her. I feel sorry for her, that she'll never have what I've had.'

'You've had nothing except a hard time.'

'With you.' She blinked repeatedly. 'C'mon, we'd better get to work before I start bawling.'

Fraser swore behind shut lips. If Lorraine had just an atom less integrity – But she was right, of course, and he was a rat for what he had briefly hoped. *Life isn't a story book,* he lectured himself. *There are no happy endings. It just goes on.*

Carefully impersonal, they finished the installation. Mounted on the board was a simple deadman switch connected to the main thrust-control lever and to a battery-powered timer. An acceleration of one Ganymedean gravity provided weight for resting and adjustment.

'I guess it'll work,' Fraser shrugged, 'and possibly it won't kill us.'

Jupiter was then between him and the sun. He saw stars in plenty, so great a multitude that he needed his whole piloting experience to identify the constellations. Ganymede was visible, a tiny cold crescent. He banged computer keys, working out a vector with respect to the stellar background that should bring them to approximate rendezvous. The last terminal manoeuvres would be carried out by seat-of-the-pants, a wasteful, hazardous procedure but feasible if you had a skilled hand on the board and a lot of reaction mass to squander.

The ship throbbed under his touch. Jupiter fell behind. The first stages were rough. They could have spiralled out under low thrust, but that would have required a great deal of time, so he gave a full five gravities for several minutes. After that the *Olympia* was so far out that he could drop the acceleration to a reasonable value. Most of the crossing he made at half an Earth-gee. Besides the need to spare their bodies further abuse, he didn't want to build up an unmanageably high velocity. Course corrections were difficult enough without that.

They talked together, he and Lorraine, during the hours that followed; but what they had to say was no one else's business. Not even Eve's.

Ganymede came near. Fraser was surprised to note how little fear there was in him, and how much savage anticipation. There was something wrong about feeling guilt at killing members of another species, and none at what might happen to men as warm-blooded as himself. Well, the Ulunt-Khazul had done him little personal harm, and they had not been able to shoot back at him. Matters were different now. *Yeah, quite a bit different!*

With an angry, chopping motion he switched the ship's radio to broadcast. 'Spaceship *Olympia* calling Aurora Space Traffic Control,' he spat at the raw mountainscape rolling before him. 'Request guide beam and permission to land.'

'What? *Olympia*, did you say?' exclaimed an unfamiliar voice.

'I did.' Fraser gave his approximate coordinates. 'Your radar can find me somewhere in that vicinity. Go ahead, slap a beam on. But relax. We're headed in to surrender.'

'Wait. Can you hold on for a minute? I have to check with my superiors.'

Sure, I can wait. I may be in a mean mood, but I'm not anxious to put Lory's life back in jeopardy. And I've got to.

The radio buzzed with star noise.

'Aurora Space Traffic Control to *Olympia*. Stand by for communication.'

A second later, Swayne's curbed and bitted wrath entered his ears. 'You! What are you up to?'

'We're beaten,' Fraser said. 'We tried to lick you and failed, so we're coming back.'

'Who are you, anyway? Vlasek is with you, isn't she?'

'Yes,' Lorraine said. 'Proud to be.'

Fraser gave his own name. Anything else would have been out of character.

'How did you escape that missile?' Swayne demanded.

Fraser told him, quite truthfully. 'We landed on Jupiter,' he finished. 'You'll see, when we get close, the gas bag is inflated. We had a faint hope the Jovians might be able to help us somehow. But the radio beacon down there was out. I guess the invaders wrecked it. You've heard about that war, haven't you? We couldn't even find the city we've been communicating with, in so much territory. Our supplies got

176

near exhaustion. We decided to give up.'

'Assume an orbit and I'll send a boarding party.'

'I'd rather not,' Fraser said. 'Our air is pretty foul. We could be dead before your boat matches velocities. Give me a beam and I'll follow it down to the spaceport.'

'Um-m — no, you'll have to take your chances. I don't trust you one centimetre.'

'What the devil could we do? Attempt a suicide dive on your precious ship? A rocket would blast us before we'd got halfway. Would we have returned if we didn't want to live?'

Swayne hesitated. Fraser could almost see that thin countenance twisting in thought. At length: 'Are you so anxious to live that you'll give us the names of your confederates?'

Fraser's heart bounded. *This is it!* He opened his mouth. Lorraine shook her head and raised a finger to her faceplate.

'Well?' Swayne said. 'For people whose air is running low, you're almighty leisurely.'

'It's a hard thing to ask of us,' Lorraine said.

'I want those names while you ride down. Otherwise I'll fire on you. There will be further interrogation after you've landed.'

'Okay,' she mumbled.

Good girl! Fraser thought. *That reluctant act convinced him.*

With a radar fix now on the *Olympia,* the guide beam snaked forth and locked fast. 'Give me my right position and velocity too,' Fraser reminded.

'Naturally,' Swayne said. 'But I've further instructions for you. I don't want you landing on the field. You might be tempted to try some fancy stunt, with your jets for instance, once you're inside our radius of fire. Set down on the Sinus, a mile west of Aurora, just north of Navajo Crater, where we can keep you covered. Any deviation from this line, and we'll shoot.'

'Check,' said Fraser sullenly. 'Turn me over to Control.'

'At once. Vlasek, start giving me those names.'

With his set tuned to the tower band, Fraser couldn't hear her. He could see her lips move, and imagined he could read them. Bill Enderby? Peter La Pointe? Ellen Swanberg? *We've got to carry this off, or we've spilled their lives too.* He lost remorse in the furious activity of correcting his vectors.

The moon swelled aft as he backed down until its peaks seemed to reach through the screens. Morning lay on Aurora; Jupiter was a pale, lost crescent. The engine brawled and spouted.

'You go on straight visual in sixty seconds,' the voice told him. 'Countdown: Sixty, fifty-nine, fifty-eight –

'Zero. Over and out.'

Fraser looked upon Mare Navium, dark and barren, Dante Chasm, the fangs of the Gunnison. One day there would be a sea here. But he would be very old then. He thought of returning to Earth, and realised he couldn't. For then Lorraine must depart, and she deserved oceans and blue skies.

The ground rushed up. He mixed in a sideways thrust of steering jets, to avoid the crater that grabbed at him. *Now!* said the altimeter. He pushed the switch to extend the belly jacks. Dust boiled around him. Balanced on wildfire, he gauged his moment. This was a tricky beast to land non-aerodynamically. Couldn't be done on a larger world than Ganymede, and perhaps not even then; he had not been trained in her operation. If he cracked up . . .

'I'm not going to,' he said, cut out the main blast and applied rotatory thrust. The nose swivelled to horizontal. Steering jets gave less acceleration than gravity. The ship fell.

Shock-mounted, the wheeled jacks absorbed most of the impact. Nonetheless it rocked him. He tasted blood and realised he had bitten his tongue. So much for the big bold hero.

178

The nuclear engine continued to pulse, but silence oozed up through the noise. The dust outside settled and the sun appeared.

Lorraine unplugged her helmet set from the board, tuned to the standard frequency, and said, 'He wants us to come out at once. I told him we have gas in here, under pressure, and don't want to be blown through the airlock. So we've got time to cycle through and . . . ' Her words trailed off. She was already at work on her harness.

Fraser spent an anxious minute sighting at the *Vega*. The ship glimmered on the field, enormous even at a mile's remove. He sighed with relief; the *Olympia* was pointed accurately. He'd kept an excuse in reserve for realigning her if necessary, but Swayne was so supicious that it might not have worked. Quickly he switched the autopilot to connection with the inertial compass.

Lorraine started the timer. 'Five minutes,' she said. 'Let's go.' Her face was very white.

They entered the airlock chamber and waited for it to exhaust. A curious peace possessed Fraser. He had done what he could; the rest lay with the laws of physics. Or with God, maybe. He patted the steel beside him. 'So long,' he said. 'You were a good ship.'

Lorraine started to cry, quietly and alone.

The chug of the pump dwindled away. Fraser cracked the outer door. With no ladder to help, the ground seemed a long way off. He jumped. The landing hurt his shins.

Lorraine joined him. She touched her helmet to his. 'They're watching us from the battleship,' she pointed out needlessly. 'We'd better start walking.'

'And get incinerated by the blast? Not you!' He pulled at her arm. They bounded off toward the Navajo Crater.

'Hey, there!' Swayne's voice was brittle in their ear-plugs. 'Where do you think you're going?'

'Why, we're headed around the safety wall,' Fraser said innocently. 'You want us in town, don't you?'

179

'I want you to come straight onto the field. Quick, before we shoot.'

Some eons ago a meteorite had struck the crater. The scar was still fresh. The boulder lay at the bottom of the slope. Fraser and Lorraine plunged toward it.

A laser beam winked, intolerably bright. The lava melted where it hit. It swung after the running targets. Fraser grabbed Lorraine and threw her to the ground with himself for a shield. 'No,' she cried, 'you've got Eve . . .'

The timer completed its appointed number of cycles. A relay clicked back a catch. A spring yanked the lever coupled to the main switch. The *Olympia* leaped forward.

Someone fired a shell. It exploded yards behind the spot where the runaway ship had been. The titanic rush of exhaust gases vaporised the smaller fragments. Spreading, it raged in a fog across Fraser. The ground shuddered and kicked him. Heat clawed through his armour. Blinded, stunned, he heard a roar so great that it ceased to be noise, an unchained elemental force battering his bones.

Had the *Olympia* been less stoutly built, her jacks would have torn her open. As it was, the wheels gouged a double trail of smoke, dust, sparks, and splinters. Having been ordered to steer a straight line, the autopilot used side jets for correction, flame and fury to right and left against the volcano that bellowed aft. The men on the *Vega* had perhaps fifteen seconds to watch the dragon charge them.

There was no way to stop that onslaught. The ship from Jupiter was beneath the lowest arc of gun and missile tube sooner than a human could take fresh aim. A laser battery might have destroyed her in time. But time was not granted.

Yet the *Vega* was on battle alert, her engines warm, every station manned. The pilot threw his own switch and she blasted. At maximum thrust she lifted over the oncoming mass, poured her exhaust down upon it with a force that smashed the concrete beneath.

The gas bag disintegrated. The thinner cells in the hold of the *Olympia* gave way. Jovian atmosphere exploded into vacuum. Under that much violence, already weakened by the battleship jets and with its structural cross-bracing now gone, the surface-condition compartment split. Hydrogen came out at more than sea bottom pressure. Shrapnel chunks and boulders of allotropic ice were hurled heavenward. In airlessness and rocketblast temperatures, the water molecules crashed over to a low-density form even as they flew. The energy released could be measured, but never imagined.

A shock wave through the stone of Ganymede hurled Fraser aloft. He landed hard, with a gasp, and rolled over several times before he stopped. He scarcely noticed. Nothing could be noticed but that Luciferean burst which annihilated the *Vega*.

It was over in less than a second. The gases fled back to interstellar space. A shallow crater had opened in the field. Wreckage rained down into it. Smoke and dust puffed away, the stars glittered forth, a vast and terrible silence fell.

Fraser rose to unsteady feet and helped Lorraine up. She stared wildly at him. 'Are you all right?' asked part of him. The rest was still ringing and reeling.

'Alive, anyhow,' she choked. 'You? The town?' Frantic, she peered east against the sun. The safety wall was partly crumbled, the main radio mast bent into a grotesquerie. But Aurora herself stood firm.

'We did it,' he breathed. 'Before heaven, we did.'

'Yes. B-but . . . oh, I don't know, trumpets ought to sound for me, I suppose, but mainly I just notice how I ache, how much I want to rest – and all those poor young men, and you belonging to – Let's walk back as slowly as we can.' Her gauntlet closed on his. He was reminded of Ann.

Bill Enderby met them as they neared the west central airlock. He stopped and waited, blocky in his spacesuit. The face behind the helmet was overwhelmed by victory.

'Hello,' he ventured shyly.

'What about the garrison inside?' Fraser demanded.

'They haven't done anything,' Enderby said. 'What could they do? Swayne was aboard that ship, along with most of their buddies.' He lifted the firegun he carried. 'I took this off one of 'em. He just sat there and cried. We're rounding them up now.'

'There are still the boats on patrol duty,' Lorraine said.

'No worry. What can they do either, except come in to surrender when their supplies run low? Even if they tried to dis us, they've only got three or four small rockets apiece, okay against a spaceship but not much use at a place built like Aurora. Not that they will try. Their cause is lost, and without us they'd plain starve to death.'

Enderby drew a long breath. 'This is your doing, isn't it?' he asked. 'You two?'

'We three,' Fraser said. He didn't amplify.

'I haven't got any words for you,' Enderby said. 'Nobody does. Those words haven't been made yet. Here, uh, Miss Vlasek.' He thrust the gun awkwardly at her. 'This is a hell of a nice little piece. It's yours.'

She shook her head. 'No thanks. I don't want to touch a weapon ever again. Can you get us to a doctor?'

'Oh, Lord, yes. Anything!' Glory turned to worry. 'You're not hurt bad, are you?'

'Oh, no,' she said. 'Nothing serious. But so very tired.'

She leaned on Fraser as they approached the airlock. 'You know,' he said, 'I don't feel tired at all.' The remark was perhaps a little heartless, but he couldn't help making it when he was walking with his head lifted so high.

As Colin and Ann will walk, he thought. *It seems impossible already that I, my own poor self, had the honour of buying them that right.* He looked upward. The sun was nearing Jupiter. But Eve should have gotten here even before the eclipse was ended.

**Winner of the
1981 Nebula Award
GREGORY BENFORD**

The year is 1998, the world is a growing nightmare of desperation, of uncontrollable pollution and increasing social unrest.

In Cambridge, two scientists experiment with tachyons – subatomic particles that travel faster than the speed of light and, therefore, according to the Theory of Relativity, may move backwards in time. Their plan is to signal a warning to the previous generation . . .

In 1962, a young Californian scientist, Gordon Bernstein, finds his experiments are being spoiled by unknown interference. As he begins to suspect something near the truth it becomes a race against time – the world is collapsing and will only be saved if Gordon can decipher the messages in time.

GENERAL FICTION   0 7221 1630 6   £1.75

THE REIGN OF WIZARDRY

JACK WILLIAMSON

THE GREATEST MAGICAL ISLAND
THE WORLD HAD EVER KNOWN

Crete – the dread island of wizardry where the power of
Minos was guarded by three walls. The land where every
nine years the Minoan games decided the fate of Crete's
famed ruler. Where the winner stood to gain the hand of
Ariadne, the treasure of Knossos – and command of the
formidable Dark One's powers. So it was that the pirate,
Theseus, came to the Minoan empire, determined to
conquer and destroy. Alone he faced Minos and
Daedalus in a struggle against totally overwhelming
odds . . .

FANTASY   0 7221 9185 5   £1.50

And don't miss Jack Williamson's classic *Legion of Space*
trilogy:

THE LEGION OF SPACE
ONE AGAINST THE LEGION
THE COMETEERS

– Also available in Sphere Books.

WHAT MICHELLE REMEMBERS YOU
WILL NEVER FORGET . . .

MICHELLE REMEMBERS

by MICHELLE SMITH & DR LAWRENCE
PAZDER

The horrific true story of a five-year-old child
surrendered to the devil. Only now, with the
aid of Dr Lawrence Pazder, is Michelle Smith
able to relive the terrifying ordeal which she
suffered at the hands of a group of Satanists.
An ordeal which turned into an extraordinary
battle between innocence and evil for the soul
of a five-year-old child . . .

AUTOBIOGRAPHY   0 7221 7958 8   £1.75

WAR IN 2080

BY DAVID LANGFORD
(ILLUSTRATED)

THE SHAPE OF WARS TO COME

Since the beginning of recorded history war has been a
blight upon our species. And looking at current military
technology it seems likely that our warmaking proclivities
will flourish in the twenty-first century.

British physicist and science writer, David Langford,
spells out the progressive sophistication of armaments
from the slingshot to the neutron bomb, military hard-
ware and software of future wars in space. He examines
such 'science-fiction' concepts as planet-busters, death-
rays, ecological wars, climate control and even bionic
people able to become part of the weapons and machines.
And he considers the possibility of colonisation and of
encounters with aliens of a higher technological order,
elsewhere in the Universe.

WAR IN 2080 presents a grim and frightening picture of
a future world – which none of us can afford to ignore.

WAR   0 7221 5393 7   £1.50